THE CRITIC

"Grace, aka Mama, C̶___g ___q___ ___
cook and a canny sleuth."
—*Booknews* from The Poisoned Pen

"Imagine a charming English mystery set in the
South with all African-American characters. . . .
Charms with its descriptions of delicious food,
realistic family dynamics, and smart dialogue."
—*Publishers Weekly*

"DeLoach has successfully transplanted the cozy to
the African-American South. Her Miss Marple is
Mama." —*The Purloined Letter*

"A winning picture of southern small-town life . . .
as refreshing as iced tea on a hot summer day."
—*Romantic Times*

"A sleuth with both compassion and courage."
—*The Skanner,* Portland

"Mama is an adorable detective whom readers will
love for her southern grace, kindness, and charity.
Nora DeLoach captures the essence of small-town
life . . . just like a Jessica Fletcher story."
—*The Midwest Book Review*

"Southern honesty and grit." —*Chicago Tribune*

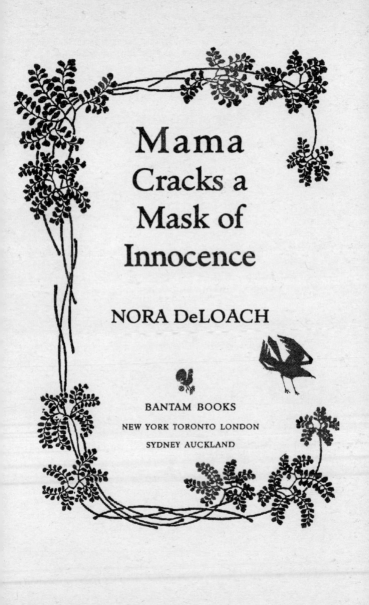

Mama
Cracks a
Mask of
Innocence

NORA DeLOACH

BANTAM BOOKS

NEW YORK TORONTO LONDON
SYDNEY AUCKLAND

MAMA CRACKS A MASK OF INNOCENCE

A Bantam Book

PUBLISHING HISTORY

Bantam paperback edition / July 2001

ISBN-13: 978-0-553-57724-2

ISBN-10: 0-553-57724-7

Published simultaneously in the United States and Canada

Bantam Books are published by Bantam Books, a division of Random House, Inc. Its trademark, consisting of the words "Bantam Books" and the portrayal of a rooster, is Registered in U.S. Patent and Trademark Office and in other countries. Marca Registrada. Bantam Books, 1540 Broadway, New York, New York 10036.

PRINTED IN THE UNITED STATES OF AMERICA

10 9 8 7 6 5 4 3 2 1

To my mother, Agatha Frazier; my brother Chester and his children, Denise, Demita, Kevin, Desha, Beverly, Chester Jr., Derek; my sister, Lurena, and her children, Sharon, Sheila, Erricks, and Spencer; my brother Victor and his daughters, Victoria and Regina.

Mama
Cracks a
Mask of
Innocence

THE MURDER

Brenda Long was dead.

Her killer glanced over his shoulder, then back down at the dead girl. His heart pounded like a caged animal's. Sweat ran down his neck. He took a deep breath, wiped his mouth, then looked down again into Brenda's face. "So you want to talk, do you?" he muttered in an effort to keep his mind focused on what he'd just done. As he'd planned, he slipped his switchblade from his pocket.

Suddenly, in the darkness and isolation, he felt exposed. Like prying eyes were nearby. He stiffened. A cat stepped in front of him and stared, a field mouse dangling from its mouth. The cat sprinted off into the darkness and he felt the sting of a mosquito bite.

The full moon, which hovered over the forest,

flashed through the trees and lit up the area. The air was quiet except for the faint sound of a foraging animal somewhere. He tightened his fingers on the knife handle.

The memory of how this Thursday began flooded his mind.

He'd awakened to the sound of his alarm clock. No sooner had he flipped the alarm off when the telephone rang. He had to answer it, he was the only one at home; his mother and her old man had gone to Tennessee for a few days. They had taken off on one of their gambling trips; their club having chartered a bus to take them there.

"Hello," he'd said, angry to be called at that hour.

"This is Brenda. Meet me in the cafeteria *before* first period!"

Hanging up, he'd felt tension tighten in the back of his neck. The feeling reminded him of his serpentine neck chain. He decided not to wear it or his new fourteen-karat gold bracelet. Something in the tone of Brenda's voice warned against drawing attention to himself. He was glad he hadn't driven his Jaguar around town. Nobody knew he had it because he hadn't figured out a way yet to explain how he could afford such a car.

His problem now was how to get to school quick enough to meet Brenda before classes started. His mama had driven her old Chevrolet to where the bus would pick them up. He'd have to drive Bo Pete's ten-year-old Mercedes.

2

An hour later, he sat with Brenda in the back of the cafeteria. She had thick black hair that feathered over small ears. Her eyes were oval, her nose narrow. She wore a pair of black slacks and a bright yellow turtleneck.

Students moved in and out of the cafeteria, but nobody came near them. He had a reputation—kids knew not to approach him while on campus. A few guys flipped their hand signs. He nodded absently, not caring that their gestures were a respectful acknowledgment. He was busy listening to Brenda: she was worried, by the look in her eyes.

"I'm tripping over this thing!"

For a moment, he didn't say anything. He struggled to come up with an explanation that made sense. He couldn't believe that she knew what was going on. "I don't know what you're talking about," he finally answered.

"Cut the crap," Brenda said. She picked up her black purse and pulled out a mirror.

He could tell that Brenda didn't see the fear in his eyes; she was too busy looking at her own face in the small hand mirror. She nodded as if pleased with what she saw, then she slipped the mirror back into her bag. "I'm going to turn you in to the authorities, but I know you're getting the stuff from a supplier," she said. "There's no way you could be bringing it into town by yourself. What I'm offering you is a deal. If you go with me, tell them where you get the stuff, things will go easy on you."

3

His face tightened. He held out the palms of his hands, as if he was pleading with her. "Listen, I don't know what you think you've found but—"

She waved her hand dismissively. "Cut the bull. I got my information from a teacher who gets her stuff from you."

"Girl, do you know what you're threatening to do to me?"

"If you go with me and tell the authorities where you're getting the stuff, it'll go easy on you," she repeated stubbornly.

He couldn't believe what he was hearing. The girl was serious, as serious as a heart attack. He cleared his throat. "You caught me by surprise," he said, his voice lower now. "I need time to figure this out."

"There isn't anything to figure. I'm going to the authorities, whether you go with me or not."

Scattered thoughts darted around inside his head like butterflies. "I need a little time—"

Again, Brenda waved a hand, dismissing any excuse he might offer.

He felt like a little boy, hemmed in. He shifted slightly in his seat, taking in every detail of her face as though he was memorizing it. "We need to talk more about this. Maybe when you get back from your class trip to Orlando on Sunday afternoon."

Brenda shrugged her shoulders in exasperation. He may have tried to look tough, but he was scared and she knew it. *With just a little more of a push*, she thought, he'd do what she wanted him to do. "I've decided not to go on the trip."

"When did you decide that?"

"After talking to you this morning. I can't leave town right now . . . there are just too many things I need to straighten out."

He started nervously picking at a fingernail but his expression remained harsh. In his head he was trying to figure out how he would get her to forget what she'd learned. "Okay, okay. Since you're not going with your class on its trip, we can meet after school, before you go home."

"No, not right after school." She looked around the cafeteria. "I have to take care of something else before I go home."

"Then what time can we get together?" he asked impatiently.

He's such a jerk, she thought. How could she ever have considered him a friend? She enjoyed making him squirm, enjoyed the fear she knew he felt. Her eyes strayed to the clock on the wall. "I don't know," she murmured.

"You *must* have some idea," he insisted.

"I'm going to need to straighten out this other matter."

"Five? Six? Seven o'clock?" he asked, his tone demanding and icy.

"Eight o'clock," she told him contemptuously.

"Where?" he asked.

She felt powerful. In a few short hours, she'd have the information she needed. She'd be a hero; everybody would see that she was a good girl who wanted to do the right thing. "On the west side of the Wesmart, the side where there are no lights." She added, "I've got to be careful, there are a lot of crazy people walking the streets of Otis nowadays."

He made an unsympathetic face.

"I'll get my friend to drop me off." She rolled her eyes. "Don't be late—I don't like being alone on the streets at night."

"Good," he whispered.

"Eight o'clock sharp," she repeated before she walked away.

❦

Once she was gone, he scrambled to pull his thoughts together. He looked around. Kids crowded the nearly tables. Food passed, waves of laughter washed across groups. But it was not the sound of youthful innocence that he heard: it was a sound of dollars and cents, the sound of easy money and he wasn't about to give it up.

He felt like he was choking. He had too much to lose, too much was at stake. He needed to talk things over with his partner.

He drove to the woman's house and parked. The shades were drawn and the gate into the fenced yard was closed. So was the door to the adjacent garage. He raised the latch, walked through the gate, and then knocked on the door.

The door opened and warm air pushed into his face. The woman's teeth flashed white in a sensuous smile; she was an experienced woman to whom he'd willingly surrendered his innocence.

"This is a surprise," she said softly.

He pushed past her and went inside. "We've got to talk!"

"It would have been nice if you'd called first."

"Brenda has figured out what's going on," he muttered.

The woman shook her head, frowning. "I'm sorry to hear that."

"I talked with her a few minutes ago. She wants me to tell everything!"

The woman cocked her head slightly at the help-lessness in his voice. "I'm not surprised," she replied, her voice low, concerned.

"The fool wants me to go with her to Abe," he told her, getting angrier as he did so. "I could have blown her away right there in front of all those kids!"

She reached for him and drew him into her arms. "You're so young," she murmured gently. "This is a lot for you to handle. I suppose the right thing to do is as Brenda suggests, let everything we've worked so hard to build go down the drain."

He pushed her away. "There is no way I'm going to let Brenda cause me to lose you!" As he looked at her, sensations bolted through his body. Before they teamed up, he'd been awkward with girls. But this was no girl, this was a woman, a woman who had taught him how to be a man, how to make big money.

"We did have such plans . . . ," she said hopefully.

"I'm going to meet Brenda tonight," he told her.

The woman kissed him on his neck. "I'm sure whatever you decide to do, it'll be for us, for our future."

He pulled her back into his arms, his heart beating passionately. "I may be young, but I'm wise in the way of making things happen. Brenda won't mess up our future," he promised her.

By the time he'd decided how he was going to handle the situation, it was dusk and he'd smoked a joint and drank a few beers. He'd driven into the woods and found a spot. It was behind a large pine which stood, like a twin, next to an oak and in front of a field bright with wildflowers.

At seven-thirty, he drove past the stores and shops of Chapel Street. Miss Candi Covington, a woman with prying eyes and a keen perception, stepped out of the florist shop. Their eyes met. For a moment he felt like his intentions stood out like a sore thumb. Then he remembered he wasn't driving his Jaguar, he was still driving Bo Pete's car. Miss Candi had seen him drive his mama's old man's car many times before, there was no reason she'd think he was up to something special just because he was driving it tonight.

Chapel Street was empty on his second trip. He took a deep breath to steady himself, parked and waited for Brenda. A few minutes later, she moved from the shadows and hurried toward his car. He started the motor as she slipped inside. "We have to talk first, decide just how to tell everything," he told her as he drove to the spot he'd carefully prepared.

For the next few minutes, neither of them spoke. Brenda seemed preoccupied. A few times he noticed she shook her head as if she didn't understand her own thoughts. Finally, she looked at him like she remembered what they were supposed to be doing together that night. "Are you going to the authorities with me and tell them where you're getting the stuff?" she asked absently.

His body stiffened. A strange whisper of excitement and warning hissed through his nerves. He studied her face. "Do you realize what you want me to do?"

"I don't understand why it's so hard for people to stand up and do the right thing!" she snapped, the pitch of her voice raising sharply. "Right is right and *you're* going to do what's right!"

Suddenly he felt a welling up in his chest, a knot that almost threatened to burst through his flesh. "There is no way I'm going to let you squeal on me!"

She looked as if she suddenly understood what he was planning. Brenda pulled the latch on the car door and flung herself out onto the ground. He was out of the car and on top of her quicker than she could scramble up to run. He slapped her a couple of times.

She sank her teeth into his arm.

Rage, like the winds of a hurricane, blazed up in him. He picked up a rock and slammed it into her face. Then his hands went around her throat.

As she struggled he felt her fingernails dig into his hands.

He had a surge of strength, one that gripped his hands tightly around her throat, one that kept him squeezing until her body went limp. When he was sure she was dead, he let out a breath, slashed her tongue, then buried her in a shallow grave among the wildflowers.

When it was all done, a sense of relief swept through him—he knew that everything would be all right once he got rid of the teacher who had squealed to Brenda, who had told her what he was doing to make his and his partner's life good!

CHAPTER
ONE

I'd been drafted.

The Otis County Department of Social Services annual clothing drive was over. Mama is a case manager in the county's office. This year, she'd volunteered as the drive's chairperson, then immediately enlisted me to help sort, separate, and transport donated items.

My name is Simone and I live in Atlanta, a full three hours' drive from Otis, South Carolina. Before I could report to my mother's home for duty, I had to convince my boss in Atlanta that I needed time off.

Sidney Jacoby is a prominent defense lawyer. He'd just instituted a policy of allowing up to five working days for his employees to do volunteer work. I decided to tell him that since I considered

Otis my home, it was right that I spend five days working on a community project in Otis instead of Atlanta.

At first, Sidney didn't buy it. He made it clear that his definition of community didn't extend two hundred miles from Atlanta. My boss is a handsome, well-dressed man in his mid-fifties. Most of the time he's calm, self-possessed, a man who not only pays me a good salary but supports the way I do my job. Needless to say, I like him. But I wasn't about to take his no as his final answer. I'd learned from working with Sidney over five years that he's inclined to change his mind if he's approached the right way at the right time. So, when I left his office I had one thought: How was I going to convince him that my community was Otis, South Carolina, where my family lives?

Then it occurred to me that it was a few days before Rosh Hashanah, the beginning of the holiest days of the Jewish calendar. Sidney is not Orthodox, but he does seem more benevolent around religious holidays. I made up my mind to try to get the week off by emphasizing that my service would not only be to my community but, in the spirit of the celebration of the upcoming holiday, it would be an opportunity for me to give service to my family and my friends.

When I eased back into his office and closed the door, he looked up and flashed me a brief smile that told me he'd been wondering how long it would take before I came back.

"I don't know if I mentioned that my work in Otis would be more than a community service . . . ," I began, trying to sound as noble as I could. "It would be an opportunity to give to my community, yes, but also, it will give me an opportunity to give to my friends and family. I wasn't born in that small town, but it produced my parents. I have many aunts, uncles, cousins who—"

He threw up his hands. "Take the week, Simone," he told me. "And give your mama my regards."

What I couldn't have realized, as I jumped for joy at my boss's concession, was that the time I was about to spend in Otis would hold far more sinister happenings than distributing clothes to needy citizens.

CHAPTER
TWO

I've told you a little about me, now let me tell you something about my mother. After thirty years, my father, Captain James Covington, retired from the air force. He built a house in Otis, South Carolina, the small town where he and my mother were born. Upon their return, Mama, who is fifty-three, and who is nicknamed Candi because of her beautiful, golden complexion, became the confidante of the county's sheriff, Abe Stanley. What started as a sleuthing game between the two of us, Mama and me, as we traveled in our military family, turned into a full-fledged occupation for Mama once she teamed up with Abe. Mind you, she does this sleuthing while working as a social worker at the county's department of welfare and cooking the best food in the South.

Before I reported to Otis Saturday morning, I

called my boyfriend, Cliff Roberts. Cliff is a divorce lawyer who is working hard to become a partner in his firm. Oddly, and for the first time, he seemed unhappy that I was leaving town. He usually encourages me to spend time with Mama, whom he both likes and admires. This time, he promised to come to Otis Saturday to spend the following weekend with me and my parents.

Mama had also recruited my father's cousins, Agatha and Gertrude, to help sort clothes. A little after noon, on the first day of my visit, the four of us stood in the Otis Community Center, ready to work.

Elliott Woods, a liver-lipped man with a speech impediment and a grin pasted on his face, peeked his head into the center. "M-Miss Candi, you want a b-bunch of fresh greens today? I j-just picked a mess from the garden."

"Yes," Mama told Elliott, smiling. "Drop two of your fullest bunches by the house later."

"Sure will," Elliott told her. "N-Nobody else wants a mess of these mustard greens?"

Gertrude and Agatha shook their heads.

"Y-You're missing a good eating," Elliott stuttered, turning and heading out the door.

No sooner had Elliott gone than Gertrude turned to Agatha and asked, "I suppose you've heard that Ray Raisin is back in town?"

Agatha didn't answer. She was sorting through a pile of infant clothes. I wondered who Gertrude was talking about.

"I can't help but think that Ray is up to something special coming back home after all these years," Gertrude continued indignantly.

Agatha, who is a thin woman with pecan brown skin and a self-effacing manner, raised one eyebrow slightly but made no comment.

"Talk is Ray's wife died and he's come home to find another one. Can't believe that, though. He's been away from these parts so long, most of his own people are dead and few people remember that he ever lived here."

"Sounds like you've been talking to Sarah, Annie Mae, and Carrie," Agatha said under her breath.

Sarah Jenkins, Annie Mae Gregory, and Carrie Smalls are Otis's historians—I say that because those three women know more about the goings-on in town than I think is healthy. They've been useful to Mama, at times feeding her background on people that Mama had lost contact with while traveling all over the world with my father.

"Yes, I talked to Sarah, Annie Mae, and Carrie," Gertrude told Agatha. "They want to believe that Ray is looking for a wife and one of them will be his choice, but I doubt he'd want any one of *them*. One thing I found interesting that Sarah let slip is that Ray Raisin asked about you, Agatha. Seems he wanted to know if she'd ever heard you say anything unkind about him, anything that might indicate that he'd not be welcomed at your house?"

But before Agatha could answer Gertrude, a woman

with fiery red hair and a milk-white complexion stuck her head in the door. "Is this where donated clothes are supposed to be dropped?" she asked.

"Yes," Mama replied. "Come on in, Pepper."

The woman eased inside the door. She was in her late forties, with a thin face, beautiful skin, and hair that hung to her shoulders. A muscular boy inched in behind her, carrying bulging Hefty bags in each hand. He was short and stocky, with dark brown skin and soulful eyes that lit up his face. "Where do you want me to put these?" he asked Mama.

"Over here," Mama instructed.

"All of this stuff is in good shape," the woman told her.

"Simone, do you know Ira Manson?" Mama asked me. "He's Otis's upcoming radio personality."

The boy smiled proudly.

"I'm impressed," I told him, and meant it.

"I haven't had a chance to listen to your program, Ira," Mama continued, "but I'm told that the young people enjoy having a deejay playing the kind of music they want to hear."

Ira started to say something when Pepper's bright red purse fell open and a nail file, a ballpoint pen, an appointment book, a packet of headache powders, a lipstick, and a cosmetic powder sponge spilled onto the floor. Hastily Ira bent to pick up the stuff that fell from Pepper's purse. When Pepper threw Ira an appreciative glance, he cleared his throat as if he might have been a little embarrassed.

Pepper smiled, then walked out of the center. Ira followed.

Sarah Jenkins, Annie Mae Gregory, and Carrie Smalls entered the center just as another boy around Ira's age, whom Mama addressed as Stone, dumped a bag of clothes inside the doorway. "Tootsie Long sent these," he said as he hurried back out the door.

Carrie Smalls, a tall erect woman who is, I think, the ringleader of the three women, was the first to enter the room. The fragrance of jasmine engulfed her.

Sarah Jenkins, a woman with a sickly yellow-squash complexion, and complaints of as many ailments as she can pronounce, eased in behind Carrie, the usual medicinal odor identifying her.

Annie Mae Gregory wobbled in next. I couldn't tell how she smelled since the combination of her companions' scents bombarded my sense of smell. Annie Mae is a big woman who has small dark eyes with circles around them. She always reminds me of a raccoon. When she looks at you a certain way she appears cross-eyed. "You've got a bountiful heap of contributions," Annie Mae said, surveying the piles of clothes stacked throughout the room.

Mama nodded, her eyes shining proudly.

Just then a man standing in the doorway cleared his throat. He was tastefully dressed in tailored clothes. "I understand this is where I'd find the prettiest ladies in town," he said.

"Ray Raisin!" Sarah beamed. "I knew you'd come like you promised."

Cousin Agatha shot Sarah an icy look.

Tall, brown-skinned, with salt-and-pepper brows and a head of silver-white hair, this man was one of the most gracefully-aged black men I'd ever seen. "I don't think I've met these two beautiful ladies," he said, walking up to me and Mama.

"Candi Covington," Mama said, then pointed to me. "My daughter, Simone."

He turned to me, gave me a wink, and said, "It is *indeed* my pleasure!"

Agatha cut her eyes at Ray, then walked toward the back of the room.

Ray looked back and forth between us. "Sarah told me that you're conducting your annual clothing drive," he told Mama.

"Yes," Mama said, glancing toward Agatha wonderingly. This was not what we'd come to expect from Agatha and we were both surprised by our cousin's openly hostile attitude.

"I don't have clothes to give away but I've got time on my hands," Ray said. "So, I'm volunteering my time and car to help deliver the clothes."

"That's wonderful," Mama said, throwing Ray a grateful glance. But her worried eyes strayed back to Agatha.

"No, it's a bit selfish," Ray said as if he still hadn't noticed Agatha's rude disposition. "You see, while

I'm offering to assist you, Miss Candi, I'm helping myself get acquainted again with the people of Otis. It's been so long since I've lived here, I've almost forgotten many families."

From her corner of the room, Agatha shook her head doubtfully, as if she wasn't buying Ray's story. In spite of whoever he claimed he'd forgotten, she obviously remembered him all too well.

"Agatha," Ray called out to her. "Perhaps you would like to go along to help direct me to where folks live."

I suppose, after the way Agatha looked at Ray, I shouldn't have been surprised by Agatha's response to that question, but I was floored. My father's cousin, the shy and retiring woman who handles the Covingtons' land corporation with as much professional politeness as anybody who majored in business, looked directly at Ray Raisin with such coldness I felt like putting on an overcoat. "Sarah, Annie Mae, or Carrie can take you anyplace in the three counties you want to go!" she answered contemptuously, then she strutted out the back door with an air that dared anybody to follow her.

Right after my cousin so rudely left the community center, Ray Raisin said his own good-byes and left. I felt embarrassed and sorry for the poor man. Sarah, Annie Mae, and Carrie must have shared my feelings, but they left right after he did, without lingering to gossip.

"What's going on between Agatha and Ray?" Mama asked Gertrude once the three women were out of hearing range.

"Agatha hates Ray."

"That's not Agatha's character. There must be a reason for the way she feels about him."

"If there is one, nobody knows except Ray and Agatha and neither of them will tell."

"Ray Raisin is educated?" I ventured, thinking of his distinguished manner and polished speech.

"He's a retired lawyer," Gertrude informed. "Ray was one of the first black men from around here to go to college."

At three o'clock we were tired and hungry. Sorting clothes is a tedious task and we'd only scratched the surface.

Deciding we'd done enough for the day, Mama suggested we start again Monday morning. Hattie Russell, her boss, had agreed that Mama's usual Monday workday could be used to get most of the clothes distributed.

We were in Mama's house for only a few minutes when Elliott Woods stopped by. "I-I declare, Miss Candi," he told Mama. "I had to p-put your mess of greens in the backseat of my car to k-keep other folks from buying them."

"You've got a lot of customers, do you?" Mama asked kindly. Mama likes Elliott Woods.

"G-good women like yourself," Elliott replied. "Good women who d-don't mind helping an old man with only a garden as his support."

After Elliott left, Mama quickly cleaned and cooked the greens. By seven, we had eaten supper and were enjoying a quiet evening. My parents and I were sitting in the backyard, a beautifully landscaped space. The air was pleasantly cool, a soft breeze stirred Mama's garden. My father was drinking his after-dinner beer and bragging about his dog's intelligence.

The doorbell rang. "I'll get it," I volunteered, thinking that nothing I'd seen of Midnight indicated that the dog was as smart as my father claimed.

If Agatha's exit from the community center had surprised me, when I opened the door to our visitors, I almost croaked.

Hattie Russell, Mama's boss, the director of the Department of Social Services, and Tootsie Long, a woman from the community, stood in our foyer.

Tootsie Long's presence wasn't as shocking as Hattie Russell's. Hattie was around thirty-five, short, with nice legs, a small waist, and wide, full hips. When Mama had bunion surgery, Hattie sent flowers and called her every day, but she never visited. Mama is convinced that Hattie is a caring and concerned woman who just doesn't think it's professional to visit her employees at their homes. This little idiosyncrasy of Hattie's explained why I was shocked to find her standing on our doorstep with Tootsie Long.

If my reaction to her visit affected her, Hattie didn't show it. "I hope we didn't catch anybody at a bad time," she said to me as she stepped inside and looked behind to see that Tootsie had followed.

"Mama is in the back," I said, closing the door and stepping in front of her. Hattie nodded slightly, then followed me into the living room.

I saw that both Hattie and Tootsie were seated, then I excused myself and headed for the backyard to alert Mama. My mother seemed as surprised as I'd been when I told her the names of her two visitors. "Something is very wrong," she whispered as she stood up.

I followed Mama into the living room where she greeted both her boss and Tootsie. "I must confess," she told the women, "this is a bit of a surprise."

Hattie fidgeted with her purse. Tootsie, who was about the same age as Hattie, held a large white handkerchief to her face, but I could still see the tears brimming in her eyes.

"Something awful has happened, something that we need your help with," Hattie told Mama.

Mama leaned forward. "I'll do what I can."

Hattie glanced toward Tootsie, then back at my mother. "Abe stopped by Tootsie's house an hour ago." She hesitated.

Tootsie spoke, her voice a bit muffled through the handkerchief. "A man who keeps beehives in the woods a few miles out of town found Brenda's body. She'd been strangled, her tongue split." Tears spilled from her eyes. Her body trembled as she seemed to contemplate what she'd just told us. Her daughter, her only child, was dead.

"I'm so sorry," Mama said.

Hattie took a deep breath as if she was trying to control her own tears. "They found the body Friday morning but Abe decided to call the State Law Enforcement people to work on the body before—" Her voice broke off. She looked at Tootsie. "They've got forensics experts but we—that is, Tootsie and I—have decided that no matter what SLED has to offer or what Abe does, we want *you* to find Brenda's killer, Candi."

Mama looked as if she couldn't believe her ears. "Hattie, I don't think you understand what you're asking of me."

"I certainly do," Hattie snapped. "I know what you've done to get to the bottom of things in this town and—"

Mama interrupted. "I'll be glad to see what I can do to help Abe," my mother told her boss firmly but kindly.

"Abe told Tootsie that this man from SLED, Lew Hunter, is in charge. That's not what I want," Hattie said, determinedly. "We want to hire you. It doesn't matter what SLED or Abe do, we want *you* to find who killed Brenda."

"Hattie, I'm not a detective. I don't have—"

Again, Hattie cut her off. "I have more confidence in you than Abe or fifty of those SLED people. I don't want you to think that your work at the department is your compensation for this project. I'll pay you separate, twenty-five hundred dollars now and twenty-five hundred when you find Brenda's killer."

"I don't want your money."

"Then I'll give it to your favorite charity."

"The county's fund that assists families who don't have enough insurance to provide a proper funeral for their loved ones could use five thousand dollars."

"It probably won't take but a week or two of your time, but Brenda was very special to me and I wouldn't be able to rest until I see her murderer behind bars." Hattie hesitated. "Tootsie may have been Brenda's mother, but I was her mentor. Brenda and I had a very special relationship."

Tootsie nodded.

"So, I speak for both of us when I say that Brenda was a wonderful Christian girl. She was just selected student of the month at school, was active in church, volunteered at the community center, and she won a scholarship from Wesmart where she worked part-time."

Mama stood up and walked to the sliding glass door. She looked out to the backyard where my father and his dog were playing. She turned and looked at both Tootsie and Hattie. The look in her eyes told me that she had reached a decision. "I'm not a detective. But I am interested in knowing why anybody would want to kill such a lovely young woman as you've just described."

Tootsie sobbed into her handkerchief. Hattie

breathed a sigh of relief. "Unfortunately, there are things in Otis that need exposing. For the past year, Brenda lived her life like she believed in more than professing to be a Christian. She believed in living a Christian life and seeing that others did the same thing."

"Do you have any idea who hated Brenda enough to kill her?" Mama asked.

Hattie opened her purse. "The first person comes to mind is Clyde Hicks. Eleven months ago there were several robberies at the Wesmart. Brenda suspected Clyde was behind the thefts. When Kevin Sterling, the manager of the store, set a trap, Clyde was caught redhanded. He was prosecuted and sent to prison. For months, he wrote Brenda letters threatening to kill her." She handed Mama several envelopes. "These are a few of his letters. Brenda left them with me."

"I . . . I didn't know," poor Tootsie moaned. "Brenda never said a word to me about letters, or threats."

"Clyde was released from prison ten days ago," Hattie continued. "He's back in town, and Brenda told me he'd been bothering her, threatening to cut out her tongue."

"I didn't know," Tootsie moaned again. "I didn't know. . . ."

"But there is somebody else who might have hurt Brenda," Hattie went on. "Brenda called my office three days ago. She told me that Victor Powell had raped his stepdaughter, Stella Hope. I promised to have the agency look into her allegations. Later that evening I got a call from Lurena Powell, Victor's wife. She told me that Brenda had called her about what Victor was doing to her daughter. Lurena made it clear that nothing was going on between her husband and her daughter. She begged me to drop the whole thing because Victor was raging mad that our agency was going to investigate him."

"And did you promise Lurena that you'd drop the whole thing?" Mama asked.

"Of course not! There was every reason for me to believe what Brenda told me. You and I both have investigated these kinds of complaints before, Candi. You know as well as I do the offending parent always resists an investigation. It's one of the signs that makes us look further for his guilt."

Mama looked down at the letters Clyde Hicks had written Brenda. "Does Abe know about these letters?"

Hattie shook her head. "I wanted him to get them from you instead of me since you'll be the one I'm expecting to get answers from."

Mama turned to Tootsie. "You had no idea that Clyde had threatened Brenda?" she asked kindly.

Tootsie shook her head. "No. And I don't understand why Brenda didn't confide in me. I don't work, so I'm always at home, always there for her when she needed me."

Mama nodded approvingly. "Tell me, who were the kids that Brenda hung out with, the kids who came over to your house?"

Tootsie struggled to pull herself together. She blew her nose, then said, "I—I don't know exactly. I mean she had plenty of friends."

"Who was her boyfriend?" I asked, the question slipping out of my mouth before I had a chance to hold it back. I hadn't been out of school so very long that I didn't remember that life in any high school wasn't worth a grain of salt if a girl didn't have a boyfriend. Brenda's boyfriend would be the one with the answers to questions that Mama wanted answered.

Before Tootsie could speak, however, Hattie interjected, "Brenda didn't have a boyfriend. She wasn't that kind of a girl!"

I made a mental note. As soon as my mother and I had a chance to talk about Brenda Long's murder, I'd tell her not to pay any attention to Hattie Russell's assertion, and to start her investigation by tracking down Brenda's boyfriend.

Mama again addressed Tootsie. "Okay, then let's move on to the last time you saw Brenda, the last time you spoke to her."

"I'd signed the consent slip for Brenda to go with her class on a trip to Orlando the week before. On Wednesday night when Brenda came in from work, I'd already gone to bed. Thursday morning, I heard Brenda talking on the phone in her room. By the time I got back to the kitchen, she was heading for the door—" Tootsie hesitated. "I went to her room. The bed was made up. The bus was to leave that afternoon right from school, so it

28

didn't bother me not to talk to her anymore. I mean, I never thought any more about Brenda's absence until Abe came. . . ."

Mama's brow set the way it does when her sleuthing instinct was put in motion. But there was something else. It was so slight that I don't know if Tootsie or Hattie even recognized it. To me, though, it was clear. I can only describe what I saw in Mama's eyes as a shadow of doubt.

CHAPTER
THREE

I awoke the next morning, Sunday, around six o'clock to an uneasiness in the pit of my stomach. I hesitated to get out of bed but the aroma of Mama's French vanilla coffee lured me into the kitchen. My mama was doing her thing, fixing a gourmet breakfast.

Mama has a gentleness about her that when added to the aroma of her cooking usually soothes most of my discomforts. However, when there is something heavy on her mind, she has another look, a kind of a fierce glow of what I can only describe as an inner determination. When Mama has this glow, her cooking isn't designed to soothe—it's a vehicle to organize and arrange her own thoughts. This morning, Mama was lit up—she was rolling neat little round biscuits and putting them onto a cookie sheet.

"I hope you're not worried about doing this job for Hattie?" I asked, thinking that the apprehension I felt might have been the result of knowing that my mother's boss had drawn her into another murder investigation.

"Hattie Russell is my boss but she didn't come here last night in that role."

I poured myself a cup of coffee and took a sip. I waited for Mama to continue.

"No, Simone, I'm not intimidated by Hattie. She's a fine woman, smart enough to separate my position at the agency from my helping her personally. No, it's not Hattie that concerns me," she said, puzzled. "It's Tootsie . . . Did you notice how she described herself as a stay-at-home mother, always available to her daughter? Then she said that she wasn't worried about her going out of town after not having spoken to Brenda for at least two days. There's something strange about that kind of a relationship between a child and a parent."

"I don't know about a parent-and-children relationship," I told her. "But I do know that every high school girl wants their own man. Trust me, the boyfriend is the one we need to track down; he's the one who's got the answers to questions!"

Mama finished the biscuits and placed them on a cookie sheet. "There's a notebook in the desk drawer. Get it for me. It'll help us keep track of who we talk to and what we learn."

The notebook was placed neatly on top of a few

envelopes. I took it out, and on the very first page, I wrote the date and the name, *Brenda Long*.

Mama put on her cooking mitten, picked up the cookie sheet, opened the oven and shoved the pan of biscuits inside. "First we'll talk to Clyde. Hattie will want me to do that before I do anything else." She paused. "By the way, I called Abe."

"Invited him for breakfast, did you?"

"Yes."

"I suspected as much."

When I opened the door for Abe Stanley, I could smell the cigarette smoke in his clothes. A three-pack-a-day smoker, I think he torturously denies himself the pleasure whenever Mama is around since he knows how uncomfortable she is with his smoking.

Abe is a man of sixty, with thin gray hair and an expressive face that tells you what's on his mind even before his words do.

Mama's kitchen was warm with the scent of biscuits minutes from coming out of the oven. Abe surveyed Mama's table. He saw scrambled eggs, freshly squeezed orange juice, sliced fried green tomatoes, grits, peach marmalade, coffee, sausage, and thick sliced bacon fried to perfection.

At that moment my father walked into the kitchen. "How's it going, Abe?" he asked, pulling back a chair and sitting down.

"Things could be better, although looking at Candi's table I can't for the life of me remember how!"

Daddy laughed. "Candi really put it on this morning. I tell you, my woman really knows how to cook. Pull yourself up a chair and take some weight off your feet and, of course, help yourself!"

Abe grinned, sat down, leaned forward in his chair, picked up his fork and, without moving his eyes from the food, said, "Candi, James got reason to brag on your cooking. I don't know anybody in town who can even come close to beating you for fixing a good meal!"

Mama nodded, although Abe didn't notice because he was busy filling his plate with portions of everything that was on the table.

"I'm sorry to hear about Brenda Long's death," Mama said. The words slipping out her mouth as easily as butter melted on her flaky biscuits.

Abe put his fork down. "I reckoned you're wondering why I didn't call you and let you know about that."

Mama nodded.

"Zack Garvey, the manager of the radio station, keeps a few beehives in a field about five miles out of town. Friday morning he checked his hives and found a shallow grave—a hand was kinda poking out of the earth. I decided to call in the State Law Enforcement people since they've got the people and equipment to study the site in ways that I can't. After the grave was cleared and it was positive that the body was Tootsie's daughter, the detective from SLED, a fella named Lew Hunter, promptly took over the case. It seems that Hunter talked to Brenda last Wednesday when she called the narcotics division from her high school. Brenda told him that she'd just learned that a student was selling drugs on the campus. Lew is still waiting for the autopsy report but he thinks it took place Thursday night, sometime after eight o'clock because a woman who was trying to hurry to Wesmart before it closed told us that she saw Brenda getting into an expensive light-colored car at seven-fifty-five P.M. That was the last reported sighting of the girl." He shook his head sorrowfully. "Even with that little bit of information, Lew is sure that the girl's death was drug related.

Mama took a deep breath. "Are you trying to tell me that Brenda was taking drugs?"

"No, no," Abe said emphatically. "Lew thinks that whoever killed Brenda did so because she learned that the killer was dealing drugs at school."

The look in her eyes told me she felt uncomfortable with what Abe had just told her. "Wait a minute, Abe. I wouldn't put too much into the call Brenda made to that SLED office until we get more evidence that she was on the right track. There could be other reasons for her death," Mama continued. "For instance, do you know Clyde Hicks?"

Abe threw Mama a steady look. "What about Clyde?"

"Hattie told me that Clyde threatened Brenda because she was instrumental in him spending time in jail for stealing from the Wesmart!" Mama walked over to the desk, picked up the envelopes Hattie had given her and then handed them to Abe.

Abe pushed back in his chair, flipped through a few of the letters, then put them back in their envelopes and set them on the table next to his plate. "Candi, I promise I'll get Rick to bring Clyde in. We'll talk to him."

Mama looked satisfied. "Will you let me know what you find out from Clyde?"

"I'm sorry, Candi, but this time I can't let you in on what's happening with this case," Abe answered.

Mama's eyes grew wide.

"Lew Hunter is in charge of this one," Abe said. "His methods ain't exactly like ours. He doesn't cotton to private citizens getting involved with these kinds of cases."

"I don't understand," Mama told him.

"Lew says that most people who live in small towns don't want to face the reality that drugs are becoming an intricate part of their community."

"I don't believe that Otis teens have a drug problem," Mama asserted.

"That's exactly why Lew insists on keeping things tightly under wraps until he gets the hard, physical evidence that will convince folks that there is a serious problem that needs addressing."

Mama looked speechless.

"Candi, don't take what I'm about to say personal," he said, his voice resolved. "You've been a great help to me and I ain't one to forget it. When Lew threw out his ideas they felt like a stick up my nose. But now that I've given it some thought, I'm inclined to agree that he knows exactly the way not only to find who killed Brenda Long but also get to the bottom of who's dealing drugs in town!"

CHAPTER
FOUR

I felt sorry for Mama. For the rest of the morning, she looked like she'd just lost her best friend. When Abe told her she wouldn't be in on this investigation, it took her by surprise and hit her hard. Later, as if she'd given it enough thought, her expression changed. It was after we'd eaten dinner and cleaned the kitchen. The look told me that something else was going on in her head. She made a phone call, then told me to get ready to go out for the balance of the day.

Our first stop was on Elm Street. I parked the Honda under the canopy of an old oak tree. This wasn't the first time we'd visited this place. Nothing had changed. The wood-framed, four-room house was still painted red and it was still the third of six lined side by side on the street.

We'd visited Sabrina Miley before, who is reputed to provide nighttime comfort to married men at an affordable price. I'd met Sabrina when Mama was looking into the death of another free-spirited young woman named Cricket Childs. This time, when we knocked, Sabrina opened the door and invited us right in. I took a good look at her. She didn't look more than twenty-two and there wasn't an ounce of fat on her. She had large breasts, absolutely no stomach, and full hips. She took herself seriously, like she knew her body was an investment.

The living room was cluttered, disorganized. There was a crumpled cellophane packet on the arm of the easy chair that looked like an empty cigarette pack.

While I sat looking around, Mama said, "I appreciate you talking to us, Sabrina."

"I ain't got no problem talking with you, Miss Candi. It's those old hens who can't keep their husbands in their own beds that I ain't got time for."

Mama smiled but she didn't respond to that comment. "Did you know Brenda Long?"

"Yeah, I've heard about her," Sabrina answered. "The talk is that Brenda got what she deserved because she was a self-righteous prick."

"You have any idea who might have killed Brenda or why?"

Sabrina sat down on the sofa and threw her leg across its arm. "What I heard was that some friend of Brenda was in trouble and she didn't have the sense to help him."

"Do you remember who told you that?"

"Not really. It was something I heard from somebody who was talking wherever I happened to be at the time."

Now, that's a soft-shoe around a question if I ever heard one, I thought. Sabrina was smart; she knew how not to say anything that might come back to haunt her.

"Does the name Clyde Hicks mean anything to you?" Mama asked.

Sabrina hesitated. "I've heard of him, but what I heard wasn't anything worth repeating."

"Did you hear of anybody else who may have been hanging around Brenda? Say, a friend?"

"Try a kid named Stella Hope. Maybe she'll know something that will help you."

The name Stella Hope jarred the memory of Hattie's account of how Brenda had instigated an investigation into her being raped by her stepfather. At the moment, I couldn't understand how this girl could have also been Brenda's best friend. "What about a boyfriend?" I asked, deciding that the more I learned about Brenda, the less I understood. "Did you hear whether or not Brenda had one?"

Sabrina shook her head. "I ain't heard no talk about a boyfriend, but a friend let it slip that Tootsie keeps big money in her house," she told us, pulling her leg from across the arm of the couch and

39

standing. "I guess when her husband died he left her pretty well off."

When we got into the Honda after leaving Sabrina's house, Mama asked for the notebook. I handed it to her, then sat quietly as she jotted down several notes. When she closed the book and put it back in her purse, I asked, "Where to now?"

"Clyde's house," she told me. "I'm going to have to talk to him myself. It seems that's the only way I'll find out whether or not he was near Brenda the last time she was seen alive."

"Where did you say this Clyde Hicks lives?"

"On Stony Hill near the county line."

The drive couldn't have been better. The sky was endlessly blue, with little puffs of white clouds showing up now and then.

The air was warm, with a slight breeze. We drove east, beyond a trailer park and the local Forest Service office. Then we made a right onto a narrow two-lane highway. Five miles later we'd driven past thick fields of soybeans where an occasional weathered shack with a corrugated tin roof popped up.

Following Mama's direction, I turned onto a road that was a grove of willow trees draped in shawls of moss just like green lace. We drove by a house where a couple sat on the porch. They reminded me of two people who had nothing more to do with their lives than measure time by the rocking of their chairs. Lying on the side of the road in front of their house was an old hound dog that never bothered to lift its head as we pulled to the other side of the road to keep from running him over.

"That's Bosie and Betsy," Mama told me. "I don't remember a time that I drove past their house and they weren't sitting on their front porch. And I don't remember a time when their old hound dog wasn't laying in that spot."

"I guess it's safe to say that there is no great drama going on out here."

"I don't think the people who live out here know the meaning of the word 'drama,' " Mama said. "Simone, slow down. You'll need to make a sharp left at the next road."

I slowed down and I'm glad I did. This next road was full of holes and bumps. Even though I was only doing about ten or fifteen miles per hour, I saw a quick movement off to the right and slammed on the brakes. A red fox jumped across in front of us. Then when it felt it was at a safe distance, it turned and eyed me before darting back into the brush.

It was another few minutes of bone-jarring bounces before we pulled up in front of a small white house. I turned off the ignition. The tidy little house was a traditional one-story with a full wraparound porch.

"How did you find this place?" I asked Mama.

"I've got several clients who live out here. A few of them are on our list to bring clothes to this week."

"Whenever we get back to the business of distributing the clothes, let Ray Raisin come to this part of the county," I told her. "He looks like he's got more money than I do. I'm sure I'll have to put on new shocks after this trip! Speaking of Ray Raisin, what do you think is between him and Agatha?"

Mama looked at me. "I was surprised at the way Agatha treated Ray yesterday, but right now, Simone, that's not what's on my mind."

"Okay," I said, knowing we'd talk about it when Mama was ready. I switched off the engine. Nothing moved; things were quiet, very quiet. "Should I blow the horn?" I asked, looking toward the front door, hoping that somebody would come out of the house onto the porch.

Mama sighed. "No," she said, easing out of the passenger's side of the car. "I'll knock on the door."

Without warning, my heart began to pound. "Mama, I've got a feeling that something isn't right!"

"Simone, trust me, it's okay," she said, moving toward the porch.

I got out of the car, since I was not about to let Mama go near that house without me. Just then, without warning, a German shepherd flew out from around the back of the house like a demon from hell.

Terrified, Mama stopped dead in her tracks.

I screamed, jumped back in the car, and slid behind the wheel.

Clutching her purse in front of her and using it as a shield between them, Mama faced the dog's bared teeth and warning growl with a no-nonsense air that I knew I could never imitate.

What must have been a few minutes seemed like a good hour, with the bristling shepherd glaring at Mama with pure hate. Then, slowly, the dog moved toward her.

Mama didn't move.

My heartbeat accelerated. Saying a silent prayer, I slammed both palms down on the car horn, honking it with all the force within me. *Somebody,* I prayed, *come out of the house and call off that dog!*

Mercifully, the door opened. For a moment the dog stopped moving forward and looked toward the door. Then, like a cobra striking at its prey, he lunged at Mama, zeroing in to lock his teeth into her handbag.

A voice came from the front door. "Killer," a male voice commanded. "Come!"

The dog looked up, released Mama's purse, and bolted into the house.

The front door closed without us seeing who had summoned the dog.

Mama waited until she heard the lock turn before she began to swiftly move toward the car. Once she was safely inside, she took such a deep breath that, when she let it out, I shuddered; I could feel her body tremble beside mine.

Then I tasted the blood—I'd bitten my lip. "If that was Clyde Hicks who called off the dog, I wonder why he didn't come out of the house."

Mama lifted her head and straightened her shoulders. "We'll wait a few minutes. If somebody doesn't come out to greet us, I'll try another way to talk to Clyde."

Nobody came out of the house so we finally drove away. Hours later I still trembled, just thinking about the ferocious attack of the German shepherd on my mama.

CHAPTER
FIVE

We drove home in silence. As we walked into the house and I had a chance to look into Mama's face, I knew the incident with the dog had unnerved her and she didn't feel like talking about it. I decided to make myself a cup of peppermint tea, take a bath, and go to bed.

Mama's manner was still quiet when I joined her in the kitchen the next morning. She and I had a light breakfast without my asking what was bugging her.

When we'd finished eating, and the kitchen was cleaned, Mama made another phone call. Only then did I ask, "What about the clothes at the community center?"

Mama looked a bit surprised, like she'd forgotten the reason I'd come to Otis in the first place. "We'll get back to that later," she told me. "Tootsie is expecting us in half an hour."

Tootsie Long's house was brick veneer, with four large columns. Mushroom-shaped shrubbery flanked the front porch. My hand was in midair ready to knock when the door opened. A young man stared at us.

"Stone!" Mama exclaimed.

"Miss Candi!" The clearly flustered boy hurried past us and off the porch.

Tootsie, who stood in the doorway watching the boy's quick flight, spoke. "Come in," she told us. Her voice was high-pitched.

We walked into a well-furnished living room, one whose walls had paintings hanging on it that looked like they'd come from Artistic Impressions, a company that specialized in limited editions of some of my favorite African-American artists. There were also figurines, with exquisitely hand-painted little chocolate faces. The house smelled of freshness, like it had been recently cleaned and aired.

Two days ago, when she and Hattie had made their unexpected visit, I hadn't paid too much attention to Tootsie. Hattie had done most of the talking. Without Hattie's overpowering presence, I now had the opportunity to focus on the dead girl's mother. The woman had perfect skin, as smooth as a newborn's. Her eyes shone like diamonds; although my first impression was that she and Hattie were about the same age, I saw now that I could have been wrong. With a sixteen-year-old daughter, she couldn't have been twenty-five, yet it was hard to believe she was much older. Tootsie Long was one of those women who would never grow old.

After we were seated, she sank into a navy blue La-Z-Boy chair. Tears welled up in her eyes. "I've been sitting here trying to make sense of what has happened. I'm right back where I started, you know. If it wasn't for Hattie—" She shuddered and wiped the tears from her eyes. "I'm without anybody—truly alone!"

"What about your family?" I asked.

Tootsie's wet eyes met mine. "My husband, Sonny Boy, and Brenda were my family," she told us. "They were all I had and now they are both gone!"

Nobody spoke.

"I was raised in foster homes," Tootsie continued as if it was expected of her. "I was one of those unfortunate kids nobody wanted to adopt. My caseworker told me my mother died when I was born. The state never had any contact from my father and whatever family my mother had never showed up. And now I'm alone again."

"I'm sorry," Mama said.

"I'll be fine," Tootsie said softly, twisting her handkerchief in her fingers. "Would you like to know about the first time I met Sonny Boy? That's a family portrait over there." She jumped up and reached for a framed picture that had been tastefully positioned on a nearby sofa table. "This is me, of course," she said, pointing to the woman. "And this is my Brenda and this is our Sonny Boy."

The man was handsomely dressed in an army uniform. One of his arms was around Tootsie, the other wrapped around a beautiful little girl dressed in lace, bows, and ribbons.

"The day I met him, Sonny Boy was eating barbecue at Fat Man Restaurant," Tootsie continued. "I remember thinking how handsome he looked in his uniform. I worked at Fat Man, you know. I made his potato salad and cooked the collard greens. The barbecue was his specialty. Nobody could make barbecue ribs like Fat Man!"

She looked off in the distance when she said, "You know Fat Man kept his sauce a secret although a man came by his place and offered him good money to buy it? Fat Man wouldn't sell it, he swore the secret would go with him to his grave."

"Where was this restaurant?" Mama asked.

"In Jersey, the same place that handsome Ray Raisin came from. Fat Man's place was right around the corner from where I stayed with this old woman who kept foster children. She was mean, and she was stingy. She only gave us what we had to have to live, never gave us anything extra. So I asked Fat Man for a job. One time a man told me that he came to Fat Man for my greens and potato salad and not for Fat Man's barbecue. I never mentioned that to Fat Man—somehow I knew he didn't want to hear that."

She frowned. "I didn't believe the man anyway, but it was nice of him to tell me so. Anyway, the money Fat Man paid me was what I used to buy clothes and things like that.

"Sonny Boy was on leave from Fort Dix and he didn't know anybody in town. We became friends and I offered to show him around. We had so much fun: he'd make me laugh for hours on end. Sonny Boy could really make you laugh. I haven't laughed much since he died, and now—"

"It will take time to heal from the loss of Brenda, but the Lord has a way of taking care of things—you'll laugh again," Mama promised.

"We got married six months later," Tootsie continued, sniffling. "Sonny Boy was shipped overseas. He got me a room and sent me money. I waited for him. Just like I promised, I waited.

"When Sonny Boy got back to the States he was already sick. He told me he wanted to come back to Otis to live his last days. Of course I did what he wanted. It was only right since he took care of me the whole time he was overseas.

"Then Brenda came. She was a beautiful little girl, the spitting image of Sonny Boy. From the moment he set eyes on that baby, he was crazy about her. And she him. I have to admit that I was jealous at first. I guess it was because I'd always imagined that's how I would have been if my own father ever showed up.

Brenda didn't disappoint Sonny either. That child clung to him like he was her breath." Tootsie looked exasperated. I couldn't quite figure if she was confused or sad.

"It's a shame Sonny Boy died before he had a chance to see Brenda go off to college like he wanted to. You know, he had the biggest funeral I could afford," she said, with a sudden burst of energy. "Why, Sonny Boy's old high school classmates, family, friends and army buddies came to pay their last respects." Tootsie stopped talking for a half a second and her eyes shifted downward. "My life has changed so much since he's been gone," she continued, a little more somber. "But Brenda—that poor child acted like she was going to die herself the day she saw the undertaker bury Sonny Boy! I tried to take Sonny Boy's place for Brenda but there was nothing I could do. I finally faced reality: even though I had Brenda, I was by myself, just like I'd been before I met Sonny Boy. . . ."

"I was wondering whether Lew Hunter or Abe have been to see you," Mama asked.

Tootsie nodded. "They came this morning with some men to look around in Brenda's bedroom."

"Did they find anything?"

"No," Tootsie said. "There was nothing there."

"May I take a look in that room?" Mama asked.

"Sure," Tootsie agreed. "Like I told Abe, there's nothing in there, nothing to be found."

"Will you show me the way?"

Tootsie put the photograph back on the table,

then led us down a long hall. At the end was a door that led into a small but tastefully decorated bedroom. Mama and I stepped inside. Tootsie stayed in the doorway.

From where I stood, I could see a bed, a dressing table with two pieces of jewelry on it, a chair, a wicker basket full of books, and photographs of Tootsie and a man I assumed was Sonny Boy.

Mama walked inside and opened the closet door. Stacked shoe boxes, an overnight bag in a corner, pocketbooks on racks, sweaters, dresses and blouses were all in place. Mama closed the door. "This is the neatest teenager's room I've ever seen," she said.

"I cleaned the room," Tootsie admitted. "I put everything in place just the way Brenda would have put them."

For a minute Mama's eyes shifted toward the bed or dressing table, I couldn't quite tell which. Then she smiled, nodded, and stepped back into the hall. I followed.

It was almost ten-thirty when we pulled off Tootsie's street. "Where to now?" I asked Mama.

"Styles Beauty Salon," she answered promptly. "I've made arrangements to speak to Lurena Powell."

"Lurena Powell is Stella Hope's mother?"

Mama nodded.

"Will you be talking to her about Brenda's accusation against her husband, Victor?"

"Yes," Mama told me. "Why?"

"I'm not a part of the Department of Social Services," I told her. "I really don't think it's legal that I be present when you talk to her."

Mama frowned thoughtfully. "Can you stay while I talk to her if I get her permission for you to be there?"

"If she doesn't mind, I guess it'll be all right. Still, you'll need to ask her permission before you start talking about anything that's DSS-related."

"If Lurena doesn't want to discuss Stella and Victor in front of you, you'll have to sit in the car."

"I understand," I said.

The salon was empty except for one woman whose hair was done up in an elaborate French roll. "Candi, you're on time," Lurena Powell said.

"You made it clear that you wanted me in and out of here before your eleven-thirty client arrived," Mama reminded her. "Lurena, before we start talking I need to make it clear that I'm here on agency business. My daughter Simone doesn't work for DSS. If you prefer we *not* talk with her here, she can go sit in the car until we're finished."

"I guess it's all right that she stays and listens. The news is already all over town. I've gotten two calls from clients who want to know whether or not I'm going to throw Victor out now that he's raped Stella. It's crazy, especially since there ain't no truth to any of what's being said." She glanced toward me, then back at Mama. "Both of you, come on in the back, have a cup of coffee."

Mama and I followed her to a small card table and three chairs placed against an empty wall. "This is my so-called office," Lurena said, a bit of arrogance in her voice. She poured three cups of coffee from a pot heated on a hot plate.

When she finished, Lurena lowered herself onto the chair. "I don't know how much you know about Brenda Long," she began, "but she was a very confused girl. She had this arrogant, judgmental air about her. But Brenda wasn't always the difficult person she ended up being. Up until about a year ago, she was bright and cheerful. I felt kind of close to her because she looked so much like her father. Did anybody tell you that me and Sonny Boy finished school together?"

"No," Mama answered.

Lurena blushed. "For a while, me and Sonny Boy liked each other. I thought we would really get close, but somebody else came into his life. He forgot about me, left town to join the army. I met Victor through Sonny Boy. Well, not exactly, but in a way. You see, Victor and Sonny Boy were army buddies. Victor had come to town a few times before Sonny Boy died, but when he attended Sonny Boy's funeral we started talking to each other."

"You said that it was about a year ago you noticed a change in Brenda?" Mama asked, bringing Lurena's thoughts back to what she was really interested in knowing.

Lurena took a deep, weary breath. "Candi, believe me, one year ago I would have never suspected that Brenda would go to Hattie Russell with this story about Victor and Stella."

Mama's brow knitted. "You don't believe your daughter was molested?"

"Victor didn't bother my Stella. My daughter is a typical teenager who wants her way all the time. But she's not a liar. And she swears to me on a stack of Bibles that Victor *never* touched her that way!"

"What did Stella tell you?"

"Let me tell you how this whole thing began. On Monday I gave Stella one hundred dollars to buy clothes for her class trip. She came home with two pairs of jeans and wanted me to ask Victor for more money. I told her I'd given her all the money I was going to. She'd been complaining, trying to be hard to live with, until it all came to a head on Wednesday morning. Stella started fussing because she couldn't find the shoes that matched her outfit. Then there wasn't anything in the house to eat. Next, her room was too small. At first Victor didn't say anything to her but finally, as if he couldn't stand hearing her fuss anymore, he told Stella to cut the crap and get ready for school. Stella called Victor a name. He slapped her. She left to go to school, screaming that he'd be sorry he ever put his hands on her. When Stella got to school she told Brenda about it. That evening Stella came straight to my shop from school. She pulled me back here and she told me what she'd told Brenda, that she'd thought about it and was sorry. She told me she'd later told Brenda that she had lied but by that time Brenda had already called Hattie and an investigation was planned. When Victor got home from work and I told him, he went nuts. He stood over me when I called Hattie Russell and begged her not to go through with an investigation."

"I'll need to talk to Stella," Mama told her. "If she corroborates your story, I don't see why the whole thing can't be dropped."

"Lord bless you, Candi," she said gratefully. "It'll be good to tell Victor when he gets in from work that there won't be any investigation. Victor's a big-city man, he hates it that people know so much about each other's lives the way they do in Otis."

CHAPTER
SIX

We arrived home just in time to meet my father, who was bolting out the front door. "Gertrude called me at work," he said. "Agatha had a heart attack. I'm heading for the hospital."

Fifteen minutes later when we walked into the hospital, we met Gertrude. My cousin works at the hospital as a nurse's aide, a job that she loves because she's one of the first people to know who gets admitted at the hospital. One thing Gertrude is proud of, and she doesn't fail to let you know, is that she believes that the Lord gave her the job as a ministry to let people know when one of their loved ones has been hospitalized.

"How is Agatha?" Mama panted.

"The doctor is still with her," Gertrude told us solemnly. "I've talked to the attending nurse. The heart attack was light, they think she's going to be okay."

"When did it happen?"

"I'm not sure," Gertrude told us. "Ray Raisin was driving by and saw her dog standing over a body in the little garden on the side of her house. When he investigated, he found her."

I couldn't help but think that if Agatha had a choice of who'd found her lying out in her garden, it wouldn't have been the handsome Ray Raisin.

Mama grimaced. "You know, the nearest house to Agatha is three miles away and I'm not sure Agatha needs to be that far away from a neighbor." Agatha had never married. She lived in the house where she'd taken care of her father, Uncle Chester, until he died a year ago. "There's nobody out there to keep an eye on her."

"I've tried to get her to move in with me, but she won't have it. As a matter of fact, every time I'd mention it, she had a fit."

Mama thought for a moment. "She'll have to come with us for a while, don't you agree, James?"

My father nodded.

"Agatha is a wonderful person. She's taken care of more than one of the old folks that hang out at the center," Gertrude remarked.

"She needs somebody to take care of her now," Mama continued, "and I'll be the one to do it."

Gertrude shrugged, then turned and walked back down the hall toward the emergency room. When she returned, there was a more relaxed look on her face. "They're going to put Agatha in room twelve. We can wait there for the nurse to bring her."

Fifteen minutes later, Agatha was wheeled in and transferred to the bed. She lay with her eyes closed.

"We've given her a mild sedative," said the doctor who entered the room shortly after she was wheeled in. "She was shaken but she doesn't seem to have suffered any serious harm. I do want to monitor her for the night, however. If all goes well, she should be able to go home tomorrow morning."

Mama leaned over the bed. "Agatha, everything is going to be okay."

Agatha stirred. "Candi?"

Mama took Agatha's hand. "You're going to be all right. And when it's time to leave the hospital, we've decided to take you home with us," she told her cousin.

Agatha's dark eyes filled. "No!" she moaned.

"Yes," Mama insisted. "I know you like your independence but until you regain your strength, it's better that you stay with us."

"My dog—"

"Don't worry, we'll bring Sunshine home too," Mama assured her.

I'd forgotten about Agatha's dog. It was her constant companion. Even after Uncle Chester's death, there was something special between Agatha and her dog. Now I shook my head and wondered how my father was going to give attention to both his dog, Midnight, and the *very* pampered Sunshine.

The nurse came back into the room. "She'll be asleep in a few minutes," she told us.

Our cousin tried to smile, but the dazed look in Agatha's eyes told me that she wasn't thinking of what happened as anything humorous. "The last few hours seem like a dream," she told us, as she dozed off.

It was eight o'clock when we'd finished supper. I'd put the last plate in the dishwasher. My father, who had picked up Sunshine, worked with both dogs in the backyard. "They need to get to know each other," he told us. "It'll take some time, but it'll be fine."

After checking with the hospital to see that it was okay, Mama and I headed to the hospital to take Agatha something to eat, since most people rightfully complain about hospital food. We were not surprised to find that Agatha had visitors. Annie Mae Gregory, Sarah Jenkins, and Carrie Smalls had already gotten the news of her attack and were settled in for a long visit.

Agatha lay in her bed, her eyes closed while the women talked among themselves. From the moment I walked in, I could tell by her twitching eyelids that Agatha wasn't asleep.

But when she heard Mama's voice, Agatha's eyes popped open like a cork on a Champagne bottle. Her message was clear. She wanted Annie Mae, Sarah, and Carrie out of her room!

Mama handed me the plate that we had prepared for Agatha. "Ladies," she said motioning to her three confidantes, "would you come out in the corridor for a few minutes? There is some important business I need to ask you about."

The women were excited and it showed. They moved quicker than I thought possible. As a matter of fact, it was as if the call to board the train to heaven had been heralded. Agatha smiled, then reached for the food that Mama had prepared.

I was supposed to stay inside the room with Agatha but my curiosity got the best of me. So I left our cousin to enjoy her dinner and joined Mama and the others in the waiting room. As I expected, they were talking about Brenda Long's murder.

Carrie held center stage. "I know you'd want to know what my niece Opal told me. Opal was in Wesmart one night last week, I don't remember which night, though. Anyway, she was walking to the back of the store, on her way to the toilet, when she overheard Brenda talking to Tina, one of the other clerks. Now, Opal told me flat out that she wasn't being nosy or anything, but she did hear Brenda say that the boy who had been sent to prison for stealing from the store last year was back in town."

"I heard sometime after he was sent to Columbia," Annie Mae added, "that he told people that when he got out of prison, he was going to cut Brenda's tongue out."

Sarah pulled her handkerchief from her purse and

began dabbing her nose with it. "You're talking about that thieving Clyde Hicks, aren't you? It's no secret he had a reason to hurt Brenda Long but he wasn't the only person who would have wanted to cut her wagging tongue out of her head." Sarah looked at Mama with what I consider her effort to look innocent. "You know that I ain't one for passing news about, but I know for a fact that she had something on one of those teachers at the high school. I found out—by accident, mind you—that Brenda sent a letter to the entire school board accusing a teacher of selling drugs to the students. How I know is that my sister's boy is on the school board. When I stopped by his house the other morning, I overheard him talking to somebody on the phone. He told whoever he was talking to that something is going on at that school and the school board isn't going to stop until it gets to the bottom of it."

Mama took a deep breath, a look of concern on her face. She thought for a moment. "Ladies, I did want to ask you something about Clyde Hicks. Do either of you know any of his people, perhaps somebody who can put me in touch with the boy?"

"Dolly," Annie Mae answered quickly. "Dolly Grayson. She works at the school, one of them women who cleans up after the children."

"A janitor?" I asked.

"That's right." Annie Mae nodded. "Clyde is Dolly's sister's youngest boy. She'll know how to find him for you."

NORA DeLOACH

Mama thanked the women, then asked me to go
back in and check on Agatha. When I returned, I
gave the report that I knew Mama wanted. "Agatha
is fast asleep," I told them.

"Well, it ain't no use of us going back in her room
to visit with her," Carrie said, standing. "She's been
asleep most of our visit."

"It's the medication," Sarah volunteered. "The last
time I was in the hospital they kept me so doped up I
hardly knew who was coming and going."

I tried not to smile, remembering the last time
Sarah was in the hospital. She'd been in a stew because she had succumbed to a scam in which her
tax money was stolen. Every time we visited her,
she was begging and crying for Mama's help. It was
a far cry from Agatha's restful demeanor.

To assure Agatha undisturbed rest, Mama suggested
we walk out together. Once Carrie's Buick was out of
sight, Mama urged me to hurry. "There are a few phone
calls I must make before it gets too late."

When we got home, Mama headed straight for her
bedroom to make her calls. A half hour later she
joined me in the kitchen where I was finishing up a
cup of southern butter-pecan-flavored coffee and a
piece of pineapple upside-down cake.

"I just talked to Hattie," Mama informed me.
"She understands that I'll need to take the rest of
the week off from the office."

"I figured as much," I said. "But you know, Sidney
allowed me time off to do community service and I

just wouldn't feel good if I got back to Atlanta and hadn't seen to it that one family got clothes."

Mama smiled. "I know what you're saying, Simone. Tomorrow, after we get Agatha out of the hospital and comfortably situated, I want to go to the high school. Perhaps I can get Dolly to get a message to Clyde Hicks. I really want to talk to that young man. And I did promise Lurena that I'd talk to Stella in an effort to at least clear up whether or not Victor bothered the girl or not. If the girl is as adamant as her mother that she hadn't been molested, I'll close that case. I promise, once we get those things done, we'll get back to distributing the clothes."

CHAPTER
SEVEN

In less than an hour after her discharge, we had Agatha at our house, in our spare bedroom, which Mama calls the boys' room, since she keeps mementos of my brothers on display there.

Before lunch, we were at the high school.

Otis High School is situated on a five-acre piece of property with several trailers behind it. The campus wasn't like any I'd ever attended, yet being on school grounds reminded me of days that were fun and days when I worked my butt off to cram so that I could get an A or B+ in a subject I hadn't paid much attention to in class.

The usual glass-filled cases with sports trophies and plaques were kept in the entrance. The walls and ceiling were painted a drab green color, the floor a muddy gray. All very familiar.

The corridor was crowded with students changing class. Ira Manson, Otis's new deejay, slipped by us, his clothes disheveled, his face bruised, like he'd been in a fight. Mama called to him and he walked toward us, his manner reluctant. "Are you all right?" she asked him.

"I'm fine," he said, pouting.

"Listen, Ira," Mama said to him, "this may not be a good time, but I need to ask you about Brenda Long."

Ira's eyes grew hostile. "What about Brenda?"

"Do you know whether or not she had a boyfriend?"

His laugh had a nasty tone. "Are you kidding, Miss Candi? No decent boy in the world would get near that holier-than-thou liar. I ain't saying Brenda deserved to get killed, but I know why whoever did it cut her lying tongue out."

Mama changed the subject. "I'm looking for Dolly Grayson," she told him. "Do you have any idea where I can find her?"

"Look in the last room at the end of this hall," Ira told Mama. "I saw her there a few minutes ago. I've got to go home," he added angrily.

Dolly was a woman who could have been a lot more attractive had it not been for the puckered worry lines in her forehead. She was pulling wads of papers from a crammed desk. "Dolly, can we talk with you for a minute?" Mama asked as we approached.

The woman looked up. "Is that you, Miss Candi?"

"Yes. And this is my daughter, Simone."

"What are you doing at the school?" Dolly asked.

"I'm looking for you."

"Me?"

"I wanted to ask you about your nephew Clyde."

The expression on Dolly's face changed. "What has he been up to now?"

"I'm not sure," Mama answered. "But I'd like to talk to him. I stopped by his house on Sunday afternoon. Somebody was at home. I know because I heard the voice of the person who called off an attack from a German shepherd. Simone and I waited for a good while, but nobody ever came out of the house."

"I'm surprised that dog didn't tear you to pieces."

"He almost did," Mama admitted. "Still, I didn't get a chance to talk to Clyde."

"You think he had something to do with that girl they found dead, don't you?"

"He threatened her quite a bit."

The frown in Dolly's forehead deepened. "Clyde didn't hurt that girl. After all she'd done to him, his heart wouldn't let him do her any harm!"

"If Clyde doesn't have anything to hide there's no reason he wouldn't want to talk to us."

"He's done already talked to Abe and that man from Columbia."

"When?"

"Yesterday," Dolly told us. "That deputy, Rick Martin, caught up with Clyde and took him to jail. Abe and the man from Columbia talked with him but they decided he ain't had nothing to do with that girl's murder. Clyde told them he wasn't nowhere near Otis all last week. My brother's wife has a sister in North Carolina who is dying with cancer. Clyde left here last Sunday to go see her, and he didn't get back to town until late Saturday night. Miss Candi, I know Clyde did something our family ain't proud of, but he wouldn't have hurt that girl."

"He threatened her."

"He just wanted to scare her. Besides," Dolly argued, "Clyde wasn't the only one that girl's wagging tongue hurt. I overheard two of the teachers talking in the lounge. It seems that Brenda Long sent a letter to the school board saying that one of the teachers was selling drugs to the students. Now, if I was that teacher, I'd certainly want to stop talk like that, don't you think?"

Mama looked interested. Dolly's story corroborated what Sarah had told us the night before.

Dolly continued. "I don't know who that teacher selling drugs is, but I've got an idea. If she didn't do the killing herself, I bet she knows exactly who did."

"Do you have a teacher in mind?" Mama asked. "Why do you say *she*? Is it a woman?"

"Mind you, this is only speculation—I ain't got no evidence to prove me right. If I give you a name, you promise not to put it to me or what we're talking about?"

Mama nodded.

Dolly whispered a few words in Mama's ear.

"Like I told you, Candi, I ain't got no proof it's her. It's just that I've seen something that I don't quite understand. Now, I know I ain't had the education like the teachers, but I've got common sense, don't you think?"

"Yes," Mama agreed.

"Common sense tells me that I've seen this person do something that doesn't sit right."

"What did you see?"

"You promise not to get me involved?"

"I promise."

"If I was a high school teacher, I'd think twice about having a good time at night with one of my students."

"Are you talking about a teacher enjoying a basketball or football game with a student?"

"I'm talking about partying down with liquor and other stuff at a club not twenty miles this side of Columbia. Now, I ain't saying I saw her sell anything but I know for a fact she was acting like she was *stoned* on something!"

"Did you tell Abe this?"

Dolly became apprehensive. "No, and if you tell him what I just told you, I'll deny saying it. This is my job. I ain't about to accuse somebody of something that might make me lose it."

"Listen," Mama said gently. "I'll pay this teacher a little visit, just to talk to her. I won't mention your name or what you just told me. If I find something out, I won't let Abe know you put me on to it. How does that sound?"

"As long as my name ain't mentioned, I don't care what you do."

"Good. Now tell me, where does this person live?"

"She's renting a house near Cypress Creek, less than a half mile from Vera Coffee, your cousin Agatha's nearest neighbor. Like I said, if you tell her I told you anything, I'll deny it. This is my job. I'm not doing anything that will cause me to lose it."

"I promise nothing will be said that will link you to her," Mama assured her. "By the way, do you know Stella Hope?"

"That girl who is supposed to be sleeping with her stepfather?"

"So that's already circulated around the campus." Mama scowled.

Dolly looked embarrassed. "Stella came to school today but ain't here now," she told us. "About a half hour ago, somebody started jabbing her about what went on between her and her daddy. That girl went home crying like a baby. I saw her leave myself. Listen, since you're here, I had to clean out that dead girl's locker. Got her stuff for her mama. If you don't mind, how about dropping it off at Tootsie's house? It'll save me a trip since I live on the other end of the county. Your house is not too far from hers, ain't that right?"

"I'll be glad to drop the things off, but Abe will want to take a look at them first."

"Abe and that man from SLED already looked at these things. The principal told me to see that they get to Tootsie's house."

"I'll drop them off."

Dolly walked away. When she returned, she had an armful of textbooks, spiral pads, and looseleaf binders. As she handed me the books, a wallet-sized photograph of three boys standing around a pool table fell out. Mama picked up the picture, glanced at it, then put it in her purse.

"I'll see to it that Toosie gets these things," Mama told Dolly.

We went home to check on Agatha. She was sound asleep, and Midnight and Sunshine were quiet.

CHAPTER

EIGHT

Mama called Lurena Powell at her beauty shop. Lurena confirmed that Stella had come home from school early and that the girl was very upset. Lurena agreed with my mother that it was a good time for us to visit her daughter.

Lurena's house was painted white with black shutters. When we arrived, Stella was looking out the screen door.

She greeted us, opened the door, and invited us inside. We followed her into a large living room with off-white walls. There was a black-and-white couch, a leather recliner, a wooden table behind the couch that had pictures of Stella and her mother, an upholstered chair, and a big-screen television and VCR. There were only two windows in the room;

both looked out onto the porch. The floor was gleaming polished hardwood.

Stella's dark complexion was smooth. She was a bit overweight, had high cheekbones and wore a dark lipstick. She was wearing a white Polo shirt, a pair of jeans and white sandals. Her nails had acrylic tips, on her left index finger was a class ring.

"That's a lovely class ring," Mama told Stella.

Stella held her hand so that the light could illuminate the ring's topaz stone. Irritation crossed her face. "I wanted Mama to get the money from Victor to buy the ring with the diamond in its center, but she wouldn't do it!"

Her words made me wonder whether this was the tone she'd used when her stepfather slapped her face. If it was, I understood his anger.

We sat down. "Come sit next to me," Mama suggested.

Stella eyed Mama suspiciously, then crossed over to the window. "I'm okay standing here," she replied.

"Before we get started talking about my reason for this visit, Stella, I need to tell you that my daughter Simone is not a part of the agency. If you choose, she doesn't have to be present while we talk. Would you like Simone to leave?"

Stella turned and stared at me. Then she shrugged. "I guess it's okay if she stays."

Nothing about her gave me the impression that she was the type who could be taken advantage of by her stepfather. Then, like the fall of a curtain, her hostility vanished and Stella's eyes filled with tears. "I spent hours with Brenda trying to convince her to call Miss Russell and tell her that she'd made a terrible mistake."

Mama nodded kindly. "I'm here to help you get that straightened out," she assured Stella. "I've already talked with your mother and she assured me that Victor never tried to molest you. If there's nothing to Brenda's accusation, there's no reason that the investigation can't be dropped."

Stella wiped her eyes with the back of her hand. "I'm sorry," she said, her voice now signaling that she'd decided it was in her best interest to tell Mama what she wanted to know.

"Let's start from the beginning," Mama urged her. "Tell me exactly how this rumor got started."

Stella bristled slightly. "I had a fight with my mama's husband. Victor's always on my case, always trying to make me do one thing or the other. I was mad and said something that made him slap me."

Mama looked the young girl in the face. "Stella— are you afraid of Victor?"

Stella waved dismissively. "No way! That big ape is ugly but I ain't scared of him." She picked up a leather pocketbook from a nearby chair and took out a pack of chewing gum. She offered me and my mother a piece. We shook our heads, she unwrapped a stick and doubled it into her mouth, biting down. She wadded up the gum wrapper and dropped it on the floor. "Victor ain't dumb. He's left mama and I don't think he's ever coming back to her. The only reason she married him was because he gave her plenty of money. All I asked her to do was to get money from Victor whenever I needed it, but my mama was greedy, she told me it's to our advantage if she puts the money Victor gives her into the beauty shop!"

This girl has a serious problem, I thought. *She doesn't mind using her mother to get money for her.* I was glad Lurena refused to give in to her childish demands.

"When did Victor leave?" Mama asked.

"From Wednesday night when he learned that there was going to be an investigation, until Sunday, Victor was cursing about how he didn't want nobody digging into his business. Mama tried to tell him that she'd get it straightened out but he was still carrying on like he was crazy until we got the news that Brenda's body was found. That's when he calmed down. I thought he'd decided that now that Brenda was dead, the whole thing about his so-called molesting me would be dropped. I guess Mama thought the same thing as I did because, on Monday evening when Victor didn't come home from work, she called his boss. Boy, was she surprised when the owner of the trucking company told her that Victor had quit his job early Monday morning and told him that he was leaving town for good."

"Let's get back to when you last talked to Brenda?" Mama asked, her voice giving away that she wasn't interested in the way Victor had slipped out of town like a coward.

"Thursday afternoon," Stella told her.

"Where?" Mama asked.

"Here, in this room."

"Tell me about that."

"I'll have to tell you about Wednesday night. I saw Brenda and told her that I wasn't going to Orlando with the class because my mama wouldn't get more money for me to buy new clothes. The next morning, I ran into Brenda leaving the cafeteria. She told me that she'd decided not to go on the class trip too and that she thought it would be a good idea if she came over to my house after school so that we could talk in private. She knew my mother would be at the beauty shop and Victor would be working." Stella paused. "When we got to the house I went into the kitchen to get cold drinks. When we finally sat down and began talking, I tried my best to convince Brenda that it just wasn't true, that Victor or nobody else had messed with me. I couldn't make her understand. God, she was hardheaded."

I wondered whether she thought that her mother could very well describe her demands and stubbornness in those exact words.

"Anyway," Stella continued, "I got her off my case when I told her that if they had an investigation I'd have to be examined by a doctor. I told her a doctor can tell when a girl has had sex and that after one examined me he'd confirm that I'd never

75

messed with a man and everybody would see that
the whole thing was a lie. That finally got Brenda's
attention, when I told her that she stared like she'd
been hypnotized. You'd think a smart girl like her
would have known that already."

"Let me make sure I understand," Mama said, as
if she was trying to put something together in her
mind. "You told Brenda that you weren't going on
the class trip on Wednesday night."

"That's right."

"And you told her your reason for not going was
that you didn't get the clothes you wanted."

"Right."

"Did Brenda tell you why she decided *not* to take
the trip?"

Stella rolled her eyes. "She said something about
staying in town to help a friend."

Mama looked surprised. "Ah, now, do you know
who that friend was?"

"It wasn't me," Stella said, her tone once again
going back to that of an unruly teenager. "Do you
know the kids at school are calling me one of those
nasty girls who sleeps with one of her kinfolk."

Mama cleared her throat. "How long did you and
Brenda talk?"

"We got to the house at four o'clock. Brenda
stayed until around seven-thirty, just about the time
Victor came in from work. She said she didn't like
being in the same house with him, and she had an
appointment at eight o'clock. I dropped her off."

"Where?"

"Wesmart."

"You drove straight to the store?"

"Yeah, but when we saw Clyde there, Brenda had me drive around the block a few times before I dropped her off. That was the first time she told me that when Clyde was in prison, he'd written her crazy letters, some threatening ones, and others begging her to forgive him. Brenda wasn't scared of Clyde, she just didn't want to see or talk to him."

"Stella, this is important. Clyde told Abe that he was out of town on Thursday, the day that it's been determined that Brenda was killed."

"He's a bald-faced liar—I saw Clyde Hicks on *Thursday* evening. I saw him and Brenda saw him."

"What happened after you dropped Brenda off?"

"Nothing."

"I mean, what did you do?"

"I went to Mama's shop."

"Did you tell your mother that you'd spent the afternoon with Brenda?"

"No way. Besides, it wouldn't done any good."

"It's quite possible that you were the last person to see Brenda alive," Mama said, as if talking to herself.

Stella didn't say anything.

"Did you tell Abe what you've told me?" Mama asked.

"He never asked me."

"I'll have to let him know what you saw," she told

Stella. Then Mama reassured the young girl that she would tell Hattie Russell that Victor hadn't had sex with her and that she was sure that the investigation would be dropped.

When we left Stella's house, Mama gazed out of the window for a while, like she was trying to get a fix on things. "There is something knocking around in the back of my head, but I can't figure out what it is," she confided.

"It'll come to you in due time," I told her. "One thing's for sure, Stella busted Clyde's alibi wide open when she saw him near the Wesmart on Thursday night."

"I suppose we should tell Abe that he was near Wesmart."

"Want me to stop by Abe's office before we go home?"

Mama nodded absently.

When we got to Abe's office, he wasn't in. The county council had finally approved the hire of a young lady to work in the sheriff's office as a dispatcher and secretary. Queenie was a perky young woman in her early twenties, with a wide smile and fiery red naturally curly hair. Mama left a note for Abe with Queenie saying that she had some information for him.

When we pulled into our driveway we were surprised to find Sarah, Annie Mae, and Carrie on our

78

front porch. The fierce rocking back and forth told us that our three visitors weren't happy campers.

I was so hungry, I was beginning to get a headache. The sight of these women added insult to misery. "Oh, no!" I moaned.

Mama looked at me sympathetically. As usual, she seemed to read my mind. "There are slices of pot roast, and sweetened iced tea in the refrigerator. Slice a tomato and have a cup of orange sherbet. That should hold you over until dinner."

I moaned again, but Mama ignored me this time and slipped out of the car. "Ladies," she said in greeting to her three confidantes.

"Where in the world have you been?" Sarah Jenkins snapped. "We've been sitting here more than an hour waiting for you. You know I suffer from high blood pressure. Sitting and waiting could make it go up in no time at all."

"I didn't know you were waiting for me," Mama said smoothly.

"It's about the clothes drive," Annie Mae jumped in forcefully. "You are supposed to distribute those things to people, you know. Clothes ain't doing nobody any good sitting up in the community center."

"You're using our space at the center," Carrie continued in the same agitated tone. "We can't get in to do our sewing, or have our lunch, or to play bingo until you get rid of those things from the middle of the floor!"

"Besides that," Sarah interjected, "Ray Raisin

been looking for you. He told us three or four times that he's prepared to deliver those things to people if you just tell him who to give them to."

"And we promised to help him and he's anxious for our help."

"Can't help the poor folks of Otis or Ray Raisin if the clothes that were given for their use are locked up in the center, now, can we?" Carrie demanded.

Oh, boy, I thought as I put the key in the lock and opened the front door. *Those three are here to lynch Mama.*

"Why don't you ladies come in and have a glass of iced tea?" Mama invited graciously. The sound of her voice made me conclude that she had already come up with a plan to defuse their anger. "I've got a sour cream pound cake that hasn't been touched."

That's it, I thought. *She's going to seduce them with something she's baked.*

The women immediately got up from their rockers and followed us into the kitchen like puppies who had been to obedience school.

Mama walked over to the sink to wash her hands. I headed for the refrigerator. Mama reached into the cabinet and took out three large drinking glasses. Then she slipped three dessert plates down, took the top from her Tupperware cake plate and revealed the prettiest sour cream pound cake you'd ever want to see. It was perfectly golden brown. When Mama cut the first slice, the moist cake looked as if it beckoned you to it.

Now, you know that I was hungry, so you might think I'm going overboard in coveting this beautiful piece of baking. And whether Sarah, Annie Mae, and Carrie shared my hungry state, I don't know. I do know that all three pairs of their eyes zeroed in on that cake.

Mama served the cake and iced tea then she went to check on Agatha, who had evidently gotten up, made her own lunch, and had gone back to bed because when Mama came back to the kitchen, she carried a tray with dirty dishes on it.

Sarah, Annie Mae, and Carrie ate the cake and drank the iced tea in absolute quiet, no more sniping at Mama.

I made myself a sandwich, then offered to make Mama one. She accepted.

As soon as the three women finished, Mama left her own food to cut them another piece of pound cake.

Annie Mae spoke first, since her plate was the first to be emptied. "Candi, ain't no use asking you for your recipe, is it?"

Mama smiled. "If you'd like it, Annie Mae, I'll give it to you."

Sarah looked into her now emptied plate. "No use getting it, Annie Mae. You ain't about to put flour, eggs, sugar, and butter together like Candi!"

Mama smiled, flattered by compliments of her cooking. Then she glanced up at the clock. "I really have to get supper started for James," she said to the women.

"When are you going to come to the center to get those clothes separated so we can help Ray deliver them?" Carrie snapped, remembering why she had come to our house.

"Tomorrow morning," Mama answered. "First thing tomorrow morning."

Mama had good intentions, but sometimes unanticipated things can come upon you so quickly that they can change the best of plans. What happened to my mother and me a few hours after dinner was just such an unnerving event.

CHAPTER
NINE

After our visitors had departed, Agatha came out of her room. "Old man Elliott Woods stopped by not too long ago," she told us as she entered. "He left a mess of okra, said he was sure you would've wanted him to. I thought you'd want them cooked for supper so I washed them, cut them up, and put them in the refrigerator."

"You sit down," Mama insisted, cleaning off the table. "You're not well yet."

Agatha obeyed, pulled a chair from the kitchen table and sat down. "Elliott is a talker, isn't he?" she told us.

"Elliott does have the gift of gab."

"He liked to talk my head off, going on about the women who buy his vegetables because they are so good. You'd think he was trying to get me to be one of his customers."

Mama laughed. "I suppose he was prospecting, seeing as you don't buy his vegetables."

Agatha didn't say anything.

"I was thinking about cooking some new potatoes and roast chicken," Mama told her. "You think that will suit you, Agatha?"

Agatha smiled and nodded.

"It'll suit me," I cut in, as I thought of the succulence of Mama's roast chicken. "I don't remember Elliott bringing fresh vegetables before this." The truth was that I knew very little about this vegetable man.

"Elliott is an old-timer," Agatha told me, her voice slightly breathy, soft. "His daddy and my daddy used to share farmworkers together to harvest their watermelon crops."

"Sarah, Carrie, and Annie Mae told me," Mama added, "that Elliott used to run a big, productive farm."

"That was years ago," Agatha told us. "Besides, the big farmers with company backing are the only ones that make money today in farming."

"Well, according to Sarah, Elliott wouldn't give up digging in the soil. He plants a very productive garden."

"Not that good," Agatha muttered.

Mama smiled. "He used to sell his vegetables directly to the Winn-Dixie. Then he had some kind of run-in with the manager. So he decided to take his wares directly to the customers, to women like me who buy fresh vegetables several times a week."

"If all the women who buy Elliott's vegetables

84

buy as many as Mama does," I said, "Elliott has a very good business."

Agatha coughed. "I don't buy his stuff—I've got my own garden."

I couldn't help but think that it was in her garden that she'd had the heart attack, and I opened my big mouth and said, "It might be a good idea for you to cut back on planting a garden."

In one split second Mama and Agatha exchanged looks, and I could see that I'd said the wrong thing. After a few seconds of awkward silence, Agatha yawned.

"I'd better go back to bed," she finally said, standing. "Doctor said I needed lots of rest."

Once she was back in her room, Mama whispered, "Agatha is clearly not interested in talking about cutting back on anything she does, Simone. But it's clear that the day is fast approaching when she'll have to cut back on some things if she plans to continue to live alone."

"I won't be the one to talk to her about rethinking anything," I told her.

Mama's eyebrows rose, but she didn't respond. She was pulling out a chicken, getting it ready for its roasting. I helped Mama prepare dinner. Don't get me wrong, Mama is the head chef and I'm perfectly satisfied just sitting and watching her. But you didn't have to be a Philadelphia lawyer to see that she had a little more than enough to handle at the moment. Not only was she under the gun to get results for her boss, she had a community center full of clothes to be distributed, and the care of a cousin who wasn't used to being taken care of.

I'd made the right call when I decided to help with dinner because when my mother had everything either on the stove, or ready to go into the oven, she sighed deeply. Then, without saying much more, she made herself a cup of peppermint tea and headed to a chair in the family room. The look on her face was clear—she needed downtime.

I decided to give Mama some space: I'd go ask Agatha why she treated the handsome Ray Raisin like he carried the plague.

The room where Mama had put Agatha is the one that Cliff usually stays in when he comes home with me. And it's the room where Will's basketball trophies and a wall lined with pictures of his team's successes are kept. There are also the five certificates of achievement that Rodney stacked up during the many selling contests he entered.

When I entered the room, Agatha, who was propped on a pillow and thumbing through a magazine, looked up as if she knew what was on my mind. "Don't ask me anything about Ray Raisin," she mumbled.

"You make it difficult for me not to want to know," I told her.

"It isn't anything that needs to be stirred."

"Ray Raisin is an angel, what could possibly be wrong with him?"

Agatha's eyelids fluttered, then she broke eye contact. "Angel!" She laughed. "I've seen more than one person with wings turn out to be an angel of darkness rather than an angel of light."

I sat on the edge of the bed. "Come on, Agatha, tell me the dirt!"

Agatha was silent for a moment. Then she yawned, eased down against the pillows and gestured impatiently for me to leave the room. "I'm tired. Doctor says I need rest!"

I took a deep breath and did the only thing I could do—I left the room. Instead of going back into the family room with Mama, however, I turned left to my bedroom. I wanted to speak with Cliff. When I called his office he was still in, and I got right through to him. I told him about Mama's boss, Hattie Russell's, offer to pay her to find who killed the teenager she had mentored.

"Miss Candi is at it again," Cliff said, "sleuthing out killers in little old Otis."

"We're going to visit one of the dead girl's teachers after dinner. Mama got a tip that she may have something to do with drugs on the high school campus."

"A murder and drugs—"

"And accusations of a young girl being molested by her stepfather."

"Are you sure you're in a small town? Sounds like

the city there, with all this crime. You and Miss Candi had better be careful."

"We will," I promised.

"Are you ready to come home?"

"I'm ready to see you."

"You miss me?"

"You know it."

"Well, say it—say, Cliff, baby, I *really* miss you!"

I laughed. "Cliff baby," I repeated obediently, "I *really* miss you!"

"How much?"

"I think you'd better stop while you're ahead."

Now he laughed. "You know I love you," he said slowly, like he was savoring his own words. It was words I'd heard before, but not with the same flavor.

"I love you too, Cliff," I told him.

Then, as if he'd been snatched back from wherever he suspected our conversation was going, he said, "You and Miss Candi had better be careful. You remember the last time you went snooping. You both came very close to meeting your Maker in a ditch."

"Do me a favor," I said, deciding that we'd permanently veered off the romantic trail of our conversation. "Go to my apartment, get my mail out of the box, check my answering machine, water my plants."

"Anything else your faithful and loyal servant can do for you, madam?" Cliff teased.

"Yes," I shot back. "But I'll give *that* order when you get here!"

After dinner Mama and I set out to visit Kitty Sharp, the person whose name Dolly had whispered in Mama's ear. "You know what Agatha said when I tried to get her to tell me why she didn't like that handsome Ray Raisin?" I asked Mama. We were passing Agatha's empty house: Dolly had told us that Kitty lived several miles down the road.

Mama looked at me.

"She said that she knew more than one person who wore wings who turned out to be an angel of darkness rather than an angel of light."

"I agree with Agatha," Mama told me.

"I don't care how many times she puts me off, I'm going to find out what went down between her and Ray Raisin. I can't imagine a man that fine doing anything to deliberately hurt Agatha."

The clock on the dashboard flashed nine-fifteen when we pulled up in front of Kitty Sharp's house. My headlights shone on a dark-colored Jaguar parked in front of us.

"Boy," I commented. "Who'd ever thought there would be somebody who made enough money in Otis to afford a Jaguar? There is at least one person in this town who is making some *serious* money!"

"Uh-um," Mama said, then, "Simone, blow the horn."

Nothing.

"What now?" I asked.

"If that's Kitty Sharp's car, she's home. If she had a dog, he'd've been out here by now—I'm going to knock."

I waited in the car, in case I needed to use my horn again. But Mama made it to the porch without any incident. She knocked on the open door. She called, "Miss Sharp!" After a few moments, she called me. "Simone, come on up. I hear footsteps. Somebody is inside, I'm sure of it."

I got out of the car and walked up on the porch, all the while looking cautiously for any approaching canines. Mama knocked again, but still nobody came to the door.

Then my mother pushed the door open a little bit farther, at least wide enough to be able to look inside. It was dark, the house eerily quiet, the smoke and odor of some recently burned incense seized our nostrils.

"Miss Sharp," Mama called again.

Nothing.

"There isn't anybody home," I told Mama.

"I heard footsteps," she insisted, stepping across the threshold.

"Let's not go inside," I said, reaching to pull Mama back onto the porch with me, but only to see her disappear into the dark house.

After a second I followed her. A few steps inside, I found her, standing motionless in the dark hallway. I grabbed her hand and tightened my grip. "Let's stay together," I whispered.

Mama took a few cautious steps forward, then halted. "Do you have a flashlight in your car?"

"Yes."

"Go get it," she told me.

"What about the light switch?" I asked her, puzzled.

"That was the first thing I tried. The lights didn't come on."

"Come with me," I said, tugging her hand toward me.

We stepped back onto the front porch. The peaceful countryside, the silence of the area, had suddenly taken on an ominous feeling. Although the evening was warm, I shivered. I couldn't shake the uneasy feeling that something—someone—was in that house watching, waiting.

I ran to my Honda, grabbed the flashlight from the glove compartment, then ran back to Mama.

Once back on the porch, I handed Mama the light. She slipped inside again, shining the light around the darkness. The first thing we saw was a large black coffee table. We were in the living room. Small plastic bags were stacked on the table.

"This way," Mama said, pointing the beam at a door in the back of the room. We left the living room and walked through a small hall. As we went into the kitchen, we heard another sound.

"Did you hear that?" Mama whispered.

"Yes," I said.

We peered vainly into the stream of the light.

"Miss Sharp?" Mama called again.

Still nothing.

My skin tingled.

My eyes darted, trying to focus on things that weren't in the flashlight's line.

We came upon another door. "This might be the bedroom," I whispered to Mama. "Maybe Miss Sharp is inside."

"Maybe," Mama answered, reaching for the door and opening it. We entered the room. The flashlight illuminated a large window. It was open, and a breeze blew the curtains inward. Mama turned slightly. The light shone on a king-sized bed. It was covered by a gaily-colored comforter, with large pillows.

A woman was lying in the middle of the bed. She had on a pair of beige slacks, a yellow sweater, and a pair of brown boots. Blood trickled from her mouth, her head was twisted at an odd angle, and her lips were curled in a tight smile. It was almost as if she was laughing at how frightened we were to have found her. It had to be Miss Sharp.

The silence was broken by a loud rustling outside of the window, the sound of a slamming car door, the firing of the Jaguar's engine as it sped away from the house.

"We almost walked in on her killer," Mama whispered.

CHAPTER
TEN

Wednesday morning a loud clap of thunder woke me. I lay in bed, trying not to think of Kitty Sharp's corpse. But the memory of the sound of the Jaguar racing away from the house, followed by the thought that Mama and I were in the same house with the teacher's killer, did not leave me.

It seemed hours that my mother and I sat in the Honda waiting for Abe to arrive. Mama had told me to turn on the light inside the car. "Look at this," she said as she opened her hand. My eyes rested on one of the small plastic bags we spotted on the teacher's coffee table. She also held a small clear oval stone that, to my untrained eye, looked like a diamond. It must haven fallen from a setting on a piece of jewelry.

"Do you know what that bag is used for?" I asked.

"No," Mama said, "but judging by the size, it can't hold much."

"It's used for drugs," I told her. "The word 'viper' is the street name for cocaine."

"Dolly insinuated that Kitty Sharp was a user."

"She may also have been a dealer," I said. "You shouldn't have picked those things up—they're evidence."

"Abe won't miss one bag; there are others."

"What about the diamond?" I asked. "Are you going to turn that over to him?"

Mama considered briefly. "I don't know," she said. She turned the diamond over, holding it up to the faint light. "I wish I could be sure that once I turned it over to him I'd get a chance to see it again."

"You could be charged with evidence tampering."

"Simone, the stone may not have had anything to do with Kitty's death. It could very well have dropped from a piece of *her* jewelry."

I could feel my eyes roll heavenward. Mama was smart enough to realize that anything in Kitty's house was considered evidence and that she had no business with either the plastic bag or the diamond.

Mama threw me a calculating look, one that told me she wanted these items in her possession a little longer. "Until I'm sure of their significance, I'm going keep them."

About that time we heard sirens. Abe, Rick, and Lew Hunter arrived. Next we peered out as the ambulance, its orange flashing light coming to a halt, stopped in front of the house. Two paramedics got out.

Once Rick turned on the electricity and got the lights working, things moved swiftly. He secured the perimeter with yellow crime-scene tape, then dusted for fingerprints. Next photographs were taken, the place was combed for evidence, and after the coroner arrived, the paramedics took Kitty's body to Otis's makeshift morgue housed at Zainer's Funeral Parlor.

Before any of that had taken place, however, Abe introduced us to Lew Hunter, who made it clear that he was in charge. When Hunter told us to meet him at the sheriff's office the next morning so that he could personally take our statements, I knew by his official tone that the probability of Mama turning over the plastic bag or the diamond was slim to none.

That was last night. I was safely in bed, listening to the rain and to Agatha shuffling down the hall toward the kitchen. Outside, Sunshine was barking.

Next Mama's footsteps.

Finally I could hear both women's voices. They weren't shouting at each other but it was clear that they weren't having a polite conversation.

I joined them.

"It's time for me and Sunshine to go home," Agatha was insisting.

"You shouldn't be out there alone for a few more days. You're not well enough."

"Sunshine needs to be let in the house," Agatha continued. "Sunshine is afraid of stormy weather."

"Now, Agatha, you know that I don't allow dogs in my house!"

"That's why we need to go home," Agatha told Mama. "Sunshine is *welcomed* in my house."

My father entered the room. "With the rain, thunder, lightning, the dogs barking, and you women talking so loud, the dead are going to wake up!"

"James, take me home!" Agatha told my father. "I want to go right now!"

"In this weather?"

"Sunshine's used to coming in the house when there's a storm. Candi won't let her come inside, so I want to take her home now!"

My father's eyes met my mother's. He turned to Agatha. "Do you think Sunshine would feel safer if I put her in the shed?"

"She's afraid of bad weather!" Agatha repeated.

"Perhaps an old blanket with Midnight as company would settle her!"

"She's used to coming into the house with me!"

"Candi, do you have an old blanket or two that Sunshine and Midnight could use?"

Mama went to the back of the house. My father followed her. I had put on the coffee, and Agatha and I sat at the table waiting for it to finish percolating.

Thunder and crackling lightning greeted my father as he opened the back door holding two thick blankets. He rolled his eyes, then dashed outside. Midnight and Sunshine really started to howl.

I poured three cups of coffee, holding Daddy's favorite mug ready for his return. When I heard the shed door slam, I poured a fresh cup and handed it to him the moment he pushed back inside the kitchen.

Mama started breakfast. The telephone rang. It was Cliff. I told him to wait while I headed to my bedroom for a private talk.

"There's been another murder," I told Cliff once I was comfortably seated on my bed.

"Why is it that I'm not surprised?"

"Mama and I found the teacher I told you we were going to visit. She was in her house, killed in her own bed!"

"What have you and Miss Marple found out?" (Cliff had taken to calling Mama Miss Marple since her success in solving murders.)

"Mama is baffled. She keeps saying that events are like a maze, one turn leads to another with nothing pointing to a way out."

"Sounds like you're not having fun," he teased.

"We haven't distributed one item of clothes since I've arrived," I reminded him.

"I'm coming in on Saturday morning. Catch the killer before I arrive—I don't want your mama doing anything other than cooking."

"Cliff, this is no time to be thinking of your stomach. Two women are dead."

Fifteen minutes later, our conversation was over and I was walking back into the kitchen when the phone rang again. This time it was Carrie who called. She wanted me to tell Mama that she thought it would probably be better for us to meet at the center tomorrow instead of today, since the weather report said that the rain wouldn't be ending until later today. When I gave Mama the message, she nodded in agreement.

The front door of the Otis jail opens into a small foyer. On the left side, a door leads into a room that has one large desk, one small desk, two executive chairs, two file cabinets, an old water cooler, a small table with a coffee urn on it, and four wooden chairs.

Lew Hunter was the first person we spotted when we walked into Abe's office. He was perched in the executive chair that belonged to Abe's desk. It was my guess that Abe had told Hunter how Mama had helped him out before, perhaps in an effort to impress him with her sleuthing talents, because Hunter glared at Mama, his eyes screaming that he wasn't partial to an ordinary citizen who might feel she could outwit his professional mind, talents, and resources.

To tell the truth, I was uncomfortable at first. I knew Mama wasn't impressed with this SLED agent for two reasons: first she didn't like Abe turning over the investigation to him, and she certainly didn't like the way he'd talked to us the night before. What I didn't know was how Mama was going to handle Hunter.

As Hunter stared unflinchingly at Mama, she refused to break eye contact with him until he finally looked down at papers on Abe's desk. By this time, we were seated in two of the wooden chairs. Hunter cleared his throat. "Why did you and your daughter go into Kitty Sharp's house last night?"

"The door was open."

"Did you have an appointment with the teacher?"

"No."

"Why did you go there?"

"A personal matter."

"Why did you go into the house when she didn't answer the door?"

"I heard a noise—footsteps."

"You heard footsteps *after* you'd entered the house?"

"Yes."

"Are you sure they were footsteps?"

"Footsteps," Mama repeated, glancing at me.

"Footsteps," I confirmed.

Lew Hunter took a notebook from his inside pocket and scribbled something on it. He stood up, walked across the floor in front of us and thought for a while. "You know that this teacher was suspected of selling drugs on the high school campus?"

"Are you sure about that?"

Lew took a deep breath.

Abe entered the room and handed Lew Hunter a piece of paper. The detective looked at the note, folded it and put it in his pocket.

You couldn't tell by the look on Mama's face, but I knew her well enough to know she was dying to know what he'd just learned.

"Mrs. Covington," Lew began, "I know you don't agree that these murders are tied up to drug trafficking. That's because you're naive. You insist on believing that your town is immune to drugs' influence. Let me assure you, you're wrong!"

Mama started to say something but before she could speak, Hunter threw up his hands. "That's all for now. If there is any need to talk with you again, the good sheriff here will be in touch."

Mama looked at me and instead of saying anything she stood up and walked straight out of Abe's office. I followed, happy that our interview was over.

The rain had stopped, the moving clouds clearing to show a blue sky.

I was surprised to see that Abe was behind us. When we got onto the sidewalk, he apologized. "I'm sorry, Candi. I'd hoped Hunter would have handled you with a little more—"

"Respect," Mama said, completing Abe's sentence. She looked at him like she could have said plenty more about Lew Hunter, but discretion held her back. "How are the investigations going?"

"There's a lot of information we've got, but nothing has come up yet that points in the direction of a suspect."

"Did you get my message about Clyde Hicks?"

"Yeah," he answered. "I'll see that Rick picks him up again but—" his voice trailed.

"You don't think Clyde did it?"

Abe began to stroke his chin like he was nervous. "Hunter's got a theory."

Mama walked forward a few feet. She looked back over her shoulder at her old friend. "I've got a theory, too," she told him.

CHAPTER
ELEVEN

Before we pulled away from in front of the sheriff's office, I sat for a moment, wanting to say something encouraging to Mama but my mind went absolutely blank. I couldn't think of a thing to say.

The look on her face, though, told me Mama's mind was ticking like a faithful timepiece. She laced her fingers together, making a steeple of her two index fingers, which she rested against her lips. "Brenda was cocky, she interfered with other people's lives, she miscalculated when she turned Clyde in, and he decided she'd gone too far, he killed her." Then she lifted an index finger, like a teacher who wants to make a point very clear. "That theory works until we ask, why kill Kitty Sharp?"

Mama was right, Brenda's murder was no longer an isolated event. She'd have to learn what tied the girl and the high school teacher together, and in solving one murder, she'd have solved both.

"Where to now?" I asked, ready to pull away from in front of the sheriff's office.

"Let's go home," she said, her voice low, almost like she was tired of thinking. "I'm concerned about Agatha. I don't think I handled the problem with Sunshine the way she wanted. I should have known she'd want her dog inside the house with her—I've seen him lying in her living room next to her heater so many times."

"Agatha knows you don't believe in letting dogs inside your house," I reminded her.

"Yeah, but Agatha doesn't understand how I feel. Midnight is James's dog, not mine. And it's hard cleaning up behind animals. When your brothers moved away, I hated to see them go but I was glad that I could begin to live in a pet-free house."

I laughed. "They did like their hamsters, didn't they?"

"And lizards, birds, fish—"

I tried to reassure her. "Agatha understands your feelings."

When we got back to the house, the silence was heavy and I immediately knew that Mama's intuition was right. She headed straight back to Agatha's room. I followed. Sure enough, it was empty. The bed was neatly made, everything was in place except Agatha.

On the refrigerator we found her note. Agatha

had called Gertrude, who had come and taken her and Sunshine home.

Mama took a deep breath. "Let's go out there and see how she is doing," she said.

"Before we eat?"

"Yes," she said, heading for the front door.

Cypress Creek is fifteen miles outside of Otis. Agatha's house sits on the edge of a one-and-a-half-acre wooded parcel. Off to the right is a three-hundred-acre pine forest. To the left is her small vegetable garden; beyond it stands an old barn. The front porch of her little five-room house looks out at a field of soybeans, the back porch faces another thick pine forest.

I rolled down my window a little to let the sweet air in. I like South Carolina. The long empty roads, the dense pine trees, the warm sweep of air when clouds briefly hide the sun, are all memorable.

Mama sat quietly, as if unmoved by the charm of the area she'd known since a child. After moving around with my military father, I often wondered how much I would have enjoyed growing up tucked snugly away in the tiny town of Otis.

At Agatha's house, Mama knocked, called Agatha's name, but to no avail. We heard Sunshine bark.

"Agatha is here," Mama said, walking off the

front porch and toward the side of the house. I followed.

"Sunshine!" I called out.

The dog barked, but didn't come.

We followed the sound, calling the dog's name. The barking led us to the barn, in the back of the house. When we pushed through the door we spotted Agatha's dog. Sunshine had old man Elliott cornered. The poor old man stood shivering, his hands full of turnip greens.

A few minutes later we were on the back porch in time to see Agatha come from the woods in back of the house. "What are you doing here?" she asked. "I left you a note."

"We got your note," Mama said, pointing to the shivering old man.

"Elliott, what are you doing here?"

"I c-come to give you a m-mess of greens," Elliott stuttered. "I f-figured once you cook and eat a m-mess, you'd never put a hoe in the ground again."

"I told you I didn't want your vegetables!" Agatha said.

"I—I ain't going to stop until you taste my greens. Tell her, Candi. She ain't p-planted anything as tender as my greens."

"Get out of here," Agatha said, dismissing the old man. Elliott walked away.

Sunshine's tail wagged. "You're a good boy," Agatha told him fondly. "Sunshine and me want to be home, Candi. You might as well get used to that 'cause I'm not going back with you."

Mama looked at Agatha with a special fondness. When she spoke, her voice was low, soothing. "I owe you and Sunshine an apology."

"No need talking about it. You got your rules for your house, I've got mine. Sunshine's used to my rules, that's all."

"Will you forgive me?" Mama asked.

"There's nothing to forgive. Fact is, I don't want any more said about it. Would you like a glass of iced tea? I just made it."

"Thanks," Mama said. "I could use a little something."

She served us glasses filled with sweetened iced tea. Then she patted her face with a handkerchief she'd pulled from her pocket and sat down heavily on the sofa. "Are you okay, Candi? I hope that worried look in your eyes ain't about me and Sunshine."

"I was worried that I hurt your feelings, yes."

"I told you don't give it a second thought."

"I know." Mama smiled.

"Something else going on inside that head of yours, now, isn't it?"

"I'm worried about Brenda Long's and Kitty Sharp's murders."

"Talk is Abe and a man from Columbia are looking into both of them."

Mama nodded. "I've been asked to see if I can find who killed poor Brenda."

"Who asked you to do a thing like that?"

"I'm not at liberty to say. But now that Kitty Sharp's been murdered, I feel obliged to try to get to the bottom of that too."

Agatha cleared her throat. "I just got off the phone not half an hour ago speaking with Vera. All she could talk about was Brenda and Kitty Sharp."

"Who is Vera?" I asked.

Mama looked over at me. "You remember I told you Vera lives about three miles down the road from here."

"Oh, yeah." I remember that it was the reason Mama was concerned about Agatha living alone. She felt that an intruder could easily get into Agatha's house and out again without anybody seeing him.

"I'm sorry for the interruption," Mama told Agatha. "Go on with what you were saying about Vera's phone call."

"Candi, you know that Vera doesn't live as far from the house that teacher, Kitty Sharp, rented as she lives from me. Fact is, I don't think their houses are more than a half mile apart."

"Yes, I know," Mama told her.

"Vera told me she thought she saw Clyde leave Kitty Sharp's house sometime around four o'clock yesterday afternoon. Something else Vera told me that might interest you. Her daughter, Wendy, works for the wife of the radio station manager. Well, according to Vera, Pepper Garvey—you know

Pepper, don't you? She's Zack's wife, the radio station manager. Anyway, as I was saying, Pepper uses Wendy to help tidy up her place. Vera doesn't mind because it's a job Wendy can do after school and it gives her spending money. Vera told me she ain't too ready for Wendy to go off on the weekends with the other girls who make beds in hotels off the interstate. Vera claims that the Garveys are a good-hearted white couple, two people who feel it's right to give young people work around town so they won't have to go off to make money."

"I like that notion," I said, taking the last sip of my iced tea.

"That girl who got herself killed didn't like it."

"Brenda?" I asked.

"Vera told me Wendy confided to her that Brenda wanted her to spy on Pepper. Brenda told Wendy that she suspected that Pepper and that boy that works at the station was doing things unchristian but she needed proof."

"Are you talking about Ira Manson?"

"Is that his name?"

"Let me understand this," I interrupted. "Brenda Long wanted Wendy to spy on the white woman Pepper Garvey and the black boy Ira Manson because she thought they were having an affair?"

"I'm only repeating what Vera told me." Agatha set down her glass and levered herself up from the sofa. Air sucked back into the sofa cushion, like the furniture was taking a breath. "You want me to call

Vera and ask her to drive up here so you can talk to her yourself?"

Mama waved her hands. "No, no."

"It's sad the way that boy slapped Brenda around."

"Who slapped who?" Mama asked, confused.

"That boy that worked at the station, Ira Manson. When Wendy told him what Brenda was trying to do, he jumped on the Long girl and gave her the whipping of her life."

"Ira Manson beat up Brenda Long?"

"I reckoned that's what happened. At least, that's what Wendy's mama told me. You sure you don't want to talk to Vera yourself?"

Mama stood up. "Right now, I don't want to talk to Vera but I'd sure like to talk to Brenda's mother. There's no way Tootsie didn't know the messes her daughter was stirring in."

It was late afternoon, an hour or so before supper. We pulled away from Agatha's house and headed back to town. At the corner of Lee and First Street, I turned right onto Second Street, where Tootsie lived. A white Ford Taurus was parked in front of her house. I spotted a parking space across the street and pulled in at the curb. Before I'd switched the ignition key off, Tootsie and a man walked off her porch. He carried a hefty-looking duffel bag in his right hand. He stowed the bag in the trunk and opened the car door, helping Tootsie as she got into the seat on the passenger side. He scanned the street on both sides, apparently deciding there was nothing to worry about. Then he walked around, unlocked the door on the driver's side, slid behind the wheel, and slammed the car door shut.

The man appeared to be in his forties. He was tall, well over six feet. He had broad shoulders, like a football player. His face was square, his eyes small for the size of his nose and mouth. We watched him check his reflection in the rearview mirror and start his ignition and pull away from the curb.

CHAPTER
TWELVE

Mama, who was beginning to look worn at the edges, ate supper, took a bath and went to bed.

I opted for watching television.

My father spent an evening with Midnight and several bottles of beer.

The next morning we headed to the community center. Not once did my mother mention Brenda Long, Kitty Sharp, or anybody involved with the two dead women.

With determined resolution to get at least this job done, Gertrude, Agatha, my mother, and I sorted what seemed like tons of clothes, all sizes, all styles. Just before noon Sarah, Annie Mae, and Carrie arrived.

Sarah started in as soon as she shuffled in the door. "I was beginning to think the poor people of Otis would never get these clothes. I know you've got a lot to do, Candi, but I'm half sick and I make the sacrifice to help out. I really don't see why it's taken you so long to get this job done!"

I was inclined to say something about Sarah's ill health that never kept her from doing anything *she* wanted to do, but Mama's eyes told me not to open my mouth.

Annie Mae, who had shuffled in behind Sarah and found the nearest chair to sit in, added, "I was about to tell the members of my church who contributed their clothes that their Christian duty was in vain. 'Bout to tell them to come on back and pick up their things!"

Carrie seemed to have decided not to say anything, but stood in the middle of the floor, put her hands on her hips, and shook her head.

"I've made up three lists, using three different areas of the county as the dividing line," Mama told the women in her usual pleasant manner. She reached into her purse and handed the lists to Carrie. "Select which one you ladies would like to be responsible for."

At that moment the dashing Ray Raisin eased inside the center. Sarah, Annie Mae, and Carrie snapped to attention like he was their commander-in-chief. "Why, Ray," Sarah crooned. "I declare, you're so sweet to help us and you're on time as always."

I could have gagged.

"Yes, ladies," he said smoothly as he made eye contact slowly and seductively with each of the women. "I'm ready and willing to work with you, or rather should I say, work for you."

"We're so glad you come to help," Annie Mae cooed.

"We'll take *this* list," Carrie said, taking one list and handing two pieces of paper back to Mama. I was willing to bet it was the list that would take them to the farthest end of the county.

Just then, old man Elliott Woods came in. "Got some of the b-best-looking red peppers you've ever s-seen for you," he stuttered. "I declare," he continued in a tone of complaint, "a l-lot of young people spend t-time at Tootsie Long's house."

"The kids probably volunteered to help her," Mama said, as she handed Elliott several dollar bills to pay for the peppers. "You know she doesn't have relatives here and there's a lot to be done in pulling Brenda's funeral together."

Elliott nodded, as if he was satisfied with what she handed him. "I've p-passed by there more than three or four t-times this week already and that place has got young people in and out. That Washington boy stays there so much that if I didn't know his m-mama, I'd swear he lived with Tootsie."

"I stopped by Tootsie Long's house to see if I could be of some help to her," Ray Raisin said, stepping forward. "I saw that boy Stone going into her garage. Tootsie told me he insists on helping her out as a way of showing how sorry he is that Brenda was killed."

"Elliott," Mama said. "I was wondering. Since you get around town a great deal, have you seen anybody driving a Jaguar? A black one?"

"Can't say I have."

"If you happen to run across a car like that, would you let me know?"

"Sure w-will. As a matter of fact, I'd let the whole t-town know. Car like that ain't likely to be in these parts unless somebody with money is sporting it."

Once Elliott left the center, Ray Raisin packed his trunk with a third of the clothes for distribution today, then escorted Sarah, Annie Mae, and Carrie to his car. The four of them drove off into the sunset, the women looking like contented cows. The disdainful look on Agatha's face told me she was glad they were gone.

We broke for lunch. Mama invited Gertrude and Agatha to our house where Mama took a spinach lasagna out of the refrigerator and put it in the oven. While it was baking she tossed salad, and put slices of garlic bread in the broiler. Then she took out a dish of sliced peaches sprinkled with brown sugar and cinnamon. Sweetened iced tea topped off our meal.

While we were eating, Mama made a phone call.

At two o'clock the dishes were in the dishwasher and we were walking out the door to return to the center. It took us another three hours to finish up the separation of the clothes. Then Gertrude packed her car with another batch of the clothes with the intention of starting their delivery first thing in the morning.

Once we packed the Honda's trunk with the remaining clothes that we planned to distribute the next morning, we swept the place clean. As we pulled away from the center, Mama shared her disappointment that she hadn't heard from Rick and that he hadn't picked up Clyde so she could talk to him.

After supper, while my mother scribbled something on a notepad and my father played with Midnight, I went into my bedroom and called Cliff.

"You're having company next week," Cliff informed me.

"I am?"

"A Naomi Flowers left a message on your answering machine. Seems you two went to college together. Well, Naomi's going to be in Atlanta on business. She doesn't want to stay at a hotel so she's coming to stay with you."

"Naomi Flowers," I said. "I don't remember a Naomi Flowers."

"She remembers you."

"Let me think," I said. But after a few moments I had to admit, "Nobody comes to mind."

"Maybe she called the wrong Simone Covington."

"Did she leave a number for me to call her back?"

"She sure did," he told me, then read it off to me. "Naomi Flowers," I repeated, baffled.

"Call her," he suggested. "She may be somebody in your past. Or she may have called the wrong person."

"What time are you arriving Saturday morning?"

"What time is breakfast?"

"I got Mama to agree to nine o'clock."

"I'll see you at eight-forty-five," he said, with a smile in his voice.

We talked for another half hour before we said good-bye. I walked into the kitchen. "Naomi Flowers," I said again out loud.

"Your old classmate," Mama said, looking up from what she was writing.

"I had a classmate named Naomi Flowers?"

"Sure did."

"You remember her?"

"She was tall, thin with a very bad complexion. But she loved chocolate. Every time I'd visit you, I baked a pan of brownies for her. I remember her well because she'd eat the entire pan of brownies in one sitting."

I snapped my fingers. "Now I remember! I remember, too, that she was one of those girls I vowed to make an effort to forget."

"You must have done a good job at forgetting," Mama said.

"I did a good job of forgetting her but she remembered me, remembered that I live in Atlanta, and wants to stay with me next week."

"How long will she be with you?" Mama asked, putting her pad and pencil in her purse.

"I don't know. I've got her phone number. I'd better call."

So I called Naomi Flowers. "Does your mother live near you?" she asked immediately. "Can you get her to make me brownies?" Yes, she was the girl with the bad complexion.

"My mother lives in South Carolina," I said, as if I were in Atlanta. "It's a three-hour drive."

Naomi sounded disappointed. "I know I shouldn't eat chocolate . . . ," she admitted.

"How long are you going to be in town?" I asked her.

"Three days. It's a work-related conference. I could have stayed at a hotel, my company would have paid for it. But why stay at a hotel when you got a friend in town?"

"You're right," I said, hoping I didn't sound too sad that she was so willing to save her company hotel charges.

"Anyway, pick me up at the Delta terminal."

"You need me to pick you up?"

"Yeah, Monday evening, seven o'clock. I made the reservations for that time so you'd have plenty of time to get to the airport from work."

"That was thoughtful," I said.

"My flight number is two-four-seven. Remember, I'm coming in from Kansas City, Missouri. Girl, I can't wait to see you. You still carry that weight around your hips?"

I didn't answer.

"Listen," she continued as if she didn't expect a reply, "I'm bringing a few nice dresses, so line us up someplace to party, okay? Dancing, you know the kind of place. My conference is over every day around three. See if you can get off work early enough to pick me up downtown."

"Naomi, I live in Decatur," I told my ex-classmate. "That's at least twenty-five minutes from downtown Atlanta."

"Doesn't matter. I don't have to be at the conference until ten. You can drop me off on your way to work."

"Yes," I sighed. "I work in downtown Atlanta."

"See, it'll work out fine. Girl, we are going to have a *ball*. Party, party, party. Don't forget. I'll be flying in on Delta, from Kansas City, Missouri. I'll be wearing a pair of black jeans, boots, and a white sweater. By the way, what is the weather like in Atlanta? I need to make sure I have enough of the right clothes. Don't worry, I'll bring enough to handle anything. Remember, my flight arrives at seven P.M. sharp!"

"I'll see you then," I said, the only words I could squeeze in before I hung the phone on its receiver.

Mama's smile told me she understood my dilemma. "Sounds like you got talked into a houseguest."

I moaned. "More like a teenager who needs a baby-sitter."

"I'll bake her a pan of brownies and send it with you."

"Oh, no you won't. I've got a hunch that I'm going to share a lot with Naomi Flowers while she's here and your brownies won't be a part of it."

CHAPTER
THIRTEEN

Before we started delivering our share of clothing the next day, we attended a memorial service for Brenda held in the high school auditorium. It was scheduled for the first period, so it was over by ten o'clock.

We delivered our share of the clothes, dropping off our last load to a woman whose husband had recently been killed in a fire that destroyed their home and everything they owned. The woman, who was now the single parent of six children under the age of eight, was still trying to deal with her loss. Mama and I stayed with her for more than an hour to allow her to talk about the tragedy.

It was almost four o'clock when Mama told me that she wanted to stop by the field where Brenda's body had been found. "It's over a week now since she was killed," I told her. "No doubt Lew Hunter has gone over those grounds with a fine-tooth comb."

"I know," Mama said. "Still, it won't hurt if we have a look at it."

The area was a perfect place to commit a murder. Lew Hunter had roped off the area with police tape. A shallow grave dug in a field of wildflowers, it was out of view from the highway because of a grove of trees. Despite its serenity, there seemed something ugly about this place. Mama, after standing and looking for a moment, began to walk beyond the site.

"Wait a minute! Where are you going?"

"I want to see how far this place is from the beehives. You remember, Abe told us that Zack Garvey found the grave when he checked on his hives."

"I remember now."

The walk took us past the grave to where four small hives were located. The stillness of the afternoon was profound, the fragrance of blossoms filling the air. It was in this stillness that we heard the child's voice.

"What you ladies doing?" the youngster hollered. He was about eight years old and was rolling a tire, something I hadn't seen a boy do since I was a very little girl.

"Just looking about," Mama answered him.

"Those men from the sheriff's office done looked at everything out here," he said, letting the tire drop to the ground, then walking toward us.

"You've seen the sheriff and talked to him?"

The boy shook his head. "I ain't talked, but I've seen him. My mama told me not to say a word, that she didn't know nothing about a dead girl and I didn't know nothing."

"Is your mother right?" Mama asked him.

"Mama told me she is always right," the child answered.

I laughed to myself, thinking that the boy was in for a rude awakening when he discovered that his mother had frailties that she herself didn't recognize.

"What's your name, honey?" Mama asked.

"Bubba."

"Bubba, did you happen to see anything, perhaps something that you forgot to tell your mama?"

"Nope," Bubba answered, his arms folded across his chest the way I suspected he'd seen his mother do whenever she was determined to hold her ground. "Just like my mama told me, I ain't seen nothing at all."

Just then something dropped from his pocket, a pocket that was the only sound piece on the pair of holey jeans he wore. He hastily picked it up. "I can't lose this," Bubba told us. "It's my change purse. I'm going to keep my money in it just the way my daddy keeps his money."

The small plastic bag had the word "Viper" written on it.

"Where did you get it from?" Mama asked.

Bubba pointed toward the grave, then, as if he remembered he wasn't supposed to have seen or known anything about where Brenda had been buried, he said hastily, "I don't know where I got it but I know I'm going to keep my money in it."

"Where are you going to get money from?"

"I don't know," he admitted. "Fact is, that is what I was wondering just before you came up. Now that I've got a wallet, I need to get money to put in it. I reckon I could try to work like my daddy. I wonder if he let me go to work with him on Saturday so that I can make some money."

"Don't know," Mama told him. "But I know where you can make enough money to buy you a leather wallet."

"Like the one my daddy's got?" Bubba asked, his eyes lighting up. "I always wanted one like that, one that you can put pictures in and that you can put dollar bills, and nickels and dimes and—"

Mama interrupted. "You can get one just like that if you sell me the one you've got in your hand."

Bubba looked at the plastic bag and back up at Mama. Suspicion welled up in his eyes. "How much will you give me for it?" he asked.

"Let me see." Mama took her own wallet from her purse. "I suspect a purse like your daddy keeps in his back pocket would cost about ten dollars at Wesmart."

"That's right," the boy said, holding the plastic bag even tighter now.

"And you'd need another five dollars to put in it."

"What about the part where you keep the nickels, dimes, and quarters?" he asked. "That's the part that Daddy opens when he gives me money."

Mama counted out a few nickels, dimes, and quarters. "This would be for that part of your wallet," she told him, handing him the money.

Bubba handed Mama the plastic bag, clutching the rest of the money. Suddenly a sadness swept over his face. "What will my mama say if she knew I got all this money for a little plastic bag that I picked up—"

"We'll go home with you," Mama suggested. "I'll explain to your mother that I wanted to give you the money, that I wanted you to buy a wallet like the one your father owns. We don't have to mention the plastic bag, do we?"

The boy shook his head. He looked at the money Mama had placed in his hand and grinned.

"Now," Mama said, as she put the bag and her wallet in her pocketbook. "Let's take you home, young fella, and talk to your mother!"

That little piece of business took us a half hour; Bubba's mother readily accepted Mama's desire to give her son money.

"Your hunch was right to visit the area where Brenda's body was found," I told Mama as we headed back to my car. "That plastic bag sure ties Brenda's death to Kitty Sharp's murder."

"It also ties her to the cocaine that Kitty Sharp was using."

"You think Lew Hunter is correct in looking for drugs on the campus."

"I don't want to believe he is right," Mama told me. "But neither can I believe that Brenda was mixed up in so many things and Tootsie didn't know anything about it. The more I think about her, the more I don't like the way she looked after her daughter."

"I suppose there are parents who just don't pay attention to their teenagers."

"Maybe, but I want to talk to Tootsie again about her relationship with her daughter. Since I didn't have a chance to speak to Tootsie this morning at the memorial service, I'd like to stop by now. We'll give her the books and school things Dolly asked us to deliver to her."

We arrived at Tootsie Long's house just as the UPS man was leaving. Once I'd handed Tootsie her daughter's books and we were seated, Mama told her of our earlier visit to her house and how we'd seen her leave with a gentleman. "A friend who came by to pay his respects," she said.

Mama related that Brenda had spent Thursday after school at Stella Hope's house. "It's strange that Brenda was at Stella's house until around eight o'clock that evening and she didn't call to tell you she'd decided not to go on her class trip."

"Candi, to tell the truth she might have called. I—I wasn't home that afternoon. I suppose if I'd talked to her, I would have been suspecting something was wrong when she didn't come home that night instead of just sitting here waiting for her to come back from Orlando." She paused. "Did you learn *anything* else that will help find out who killed Brenda?"

Mama shook her head. "Unfortunately not."

Tootsie let out a breath, then placed Brenda's books down on a nearby table. "You don't think it was wrong for me not to have a funeral, do you?"

"I suppose people were expecting a funeral for Brenda, especially since you had such a fine one for Sonny Boy."

"That was different," Tootsie replied, a little tautness in her voice. "I mean I couldn't go through another one like I had for Sonny Boy," she said, this time her voice a little more regretful.

Now I was surprised. The way I remembered it when she told us, she seemed elated that she could have provided her husband with such an elaborate send-off.

"I hope people in town will understand," Tootsie continued, her voice low, solemn. "Seeing Sonny Boy laying in a casket was almost too much to bear. I didn't want to see Brenda like that."

"It was nice of the principal to let you have the memorial service at the high school. It was a beautiful tribute to Brenda."

"I thought it would be a way for the kids to say good-bye. Hattie didn't much like it, but Brenda was my child and I was the one who had the final say."

"Were you and Brenda close?"

"As close as most mothers are with their daughters. Why?"

"I know this is a very difficult time for you, but I've got to mention some of the things I've found out about Brenda," Mama said softly. "I've learned that Brenda was involved in things that upset several people. One in particular was Ira Manson, the young man who deejays at the radio station. Did you know that he slapped her?"

"No," Tootsie said, a flash of irritation on her face. "Ira is such a nice boy, I didn't know that he'd struck Brenda."

Tootsie stood up and walked to the window. "My daughter was always so responsible I guess I gave her a lot of freedom. I mean, it wasn't like she was going to do anything wrong."

"Brenda was causing a lot of people emotional pain by her accusations. The last few days I've learned that Brenda was stirring up the kind of drama you see in soap operas."

"I didn't know," Tootsie said, her back still to us.

"You know that Brenda called SLED and told them that there was a student selling drugs at the high school?"

Tootsie walked over to a table and snatched a tissue from a box. When she'd wiped her eyes, her expression seemed a little hardened, or maybe irritated, I wasn't sure.

"Tootsie, are you sure Brenda never once mentioned the things she was involved in, the people who threatened her, even struck her?"

"She might have told Hattie but she never mentioned it to me."

"Brenda confided in Hattie?"

"I didn't know that Brenda was stirring up things. I didn't know that Clyde Hicks had written letters to her from prison. I didn't know she'd been in a fight with this Ira Manson. I didn't know—"

"I'm sorry," Mama said, interrupting her. "I can see we're upsetting you. I'll talk to Hattie. Hopefully, Brenda told her something that will help us get to the bottom of this whole mess."

We stood to leave.

"Is that man from SLED looking for a black Jaguar?" Tootsie asked, her eyes wide.

Mama looked startled. "How do you know about that car?" she asked.

"I—I don't know," Tootsie confessed nervously. "I guess I heard somebody say something about it when I was doing some shopping."

CHAPTER
FOURTEEN

Hattie Russell's brick house was a contrast to the wood-framed ones on her street. It had a brick-laid walk that led to a half porch and a detached garage. Mama rang the doorbell.

Hattie answered it dressed in a straight black knit dress, which made her look thinner than ever. She was barefoot, her face was drawn. She wore no makeup, not even a little lipstick.

We followed her inside an exceptionally large foyer which had a cathedral ceiling, a beautiful chandelier and shiny black marble floors. The walls were painted a soft off-white that was perfect for the five or six Afrocentric paintings that were taste-fully hung on the walls.

From the foyer we entered the living room, which was bright, with lovely floors, and green plants that were pushed in every conceivable corner where light could penetrate. There were glass and plants and sunlight everywhere.

The one piece of furniture that stood out was an oak bookcase. It had unique carvings, some kind of African symbols. The books on its shelves were lined up perfectly. I wondered if Hattie had used a ruler to justify each binding.

Then I realized how many of the photographs displayed everywhere held Brenda Long's face. I had seen pictures of Brenda in her mother's house but Hattie Russell's living room seemed inundated with the girl's face. Over an oak mantel was a large portrait painting of Brenda reading a book. Surrounding it were class pictures: in some Brenda was alone, in others with classmates. No matter how many children were in the pictures with Brenda, however, it was clear that her smiling face was what held the attraction. The smell of a botanic room freshener filled the room with a softness. It was almost as if Hattie had turned her living room into a shrine for Brenda Long.

The only thing that could be called a mess in this room was a pile of newspapers that were stacked in the corner. But they were stacked neatly.

I sat on a Queen Anne chair near the fireplace. It was upholstered in a delicate white with tiny navy blue stripes.

When Mama sat on the couch, Hattie joined her. "Would you like something to drink?" she offered.

Mama and I shook our heads, declining refreshments. There was a momentary silence, as if nobody knew exactly how to proceed.

Hattie took a deep breath and kept her eyes riveted to Mama's face. "What have you found out?" she demanded softly.

"Brenda was a Christian girl, like you told us," Mama began. "It seems that she took her values further than I anticipated."

"What do you mean?"

"Clyde Hicks and Victor Powell weren't the only people Brenda was trying to expose. It seems that she was working on uncovering who sold drugs at the high school."

"I've heard that."

"Did she tell you anything about it?"

Hattie stood and walked over to the mantel. For a moment she didn't answer. "She told me she suspected somebody, yes."

Mama looked at me, then back at her boss. "Did she give you a name?"

Hattie shook her head. "I didn't let her finish what she was saying," she replied. "Before she could tell me everything, I stopped her and insisted that she leave it alone. I thought she was getting into something that was way over her head and I told her so. I even made her promise to forget it. If I had only listened—"

"What about Ira Manson?" Mama interrupted gently. "Did Brenda tell you that he beat her up because she tried to get a girl named Wendy to spy on him and his boss's wife?"

"Ira didn't beat her up. He only slapped her. And Brenda swore that the lick wasn't hard."

"Victor Powell didn't try to molest his stepdaughter. The girl is a virgin."

Hattie turned to face us. "I'll drop the investigation."

"That's all well and good, but the accusation has broken up a marriage. . . . Victor has left his wife because he didn't want an investigation."

"He didn't go very far because I saw him and Tootsie together a few days ago. I—I'm sorry. I don't mean to sound so nasty. It's just that Brenda wanted to do the right thing and I, well, I guess I encouraged her."

"At the expense of hurting other people."

"Candi, you don't understand. Brenda was fine until her hospitalization a year ago!"

Mama shook her head. "No, Hattie, I really don't understand."

Hattie thought for a moment. "Candi, let me tell you a story. After you've heard it, you might not understand why Brenda was the way she was but you'll know why she means so much to me—why no matter what the cost or the motive, I'm going to find the person who killed her."

Hattie glanced up at the clock. It was a little cuckoo clock, very inexpensive and ornate and very much out of place for the simple decor of the room. "Brenda gave that clock to me," she told us. "It was a Mother's Day gift. I love it. You know, Candi, Brenda used to tell me that I was her pretend godmother. She used to ask me, if anything ever happened to Tootsie,

131

could she come live with me?" Hattie began pacing the floor. "Of course, I told her. It's strange how life works out. . . . I actually *wished* that something would happen to Tootsie so that Brenda could be with me. It was an evil thing to wish for, but nevertheless I longed for it." Tears welled up in her eyes. "Tootsie isn't Brenda's biological mother, *I* am! Looking back now, what happened sixteen years ago seems like a dream. But it was real—it happened when I was in college. The relationship between me and Sonny Boy started and ended in a few weeks. It was insignificant, as meaningless as a fly that lands on a window and then is off to some other place. . . ."

Hattie hesitated. "I never blamed Sonny Boy, you know. It was the first time either of us had sex. And after it was over, we were satisfied that what we'd experienced together was enough for either of us.

"I had no idea it was so easy to get pregnant. We were young, scared, and ignorant. We didn't know what to do. I wanted to finish school, he wanted to go into the service. We each felt cheated of our dreams, like we were victims. I hid my pregnancy as long as I could, then I confided in one of my teachers. I told her that I wanted to put the baby up for adoption, wanted to get on with my life. She helped me, got me in touch with a home for unwed mothers, where I stayed until the baby was born. My baby girl was put into a foster home and I went back to school and pretended that it never happened.

"When Sonny Boy showed up a few years later and

wanted the little girl, I helped him get her since she was still in the foster home and hadn't been adopted. He told me that he had married, that his wife couldn't have children and that she wanted his child."

Hattie crossed her arms like she was hugging herself. "It seemed the right thing to do. Sonny Boy and his wife, Tootsie, adopted little Brenda, and I lost touch with them.

"It turned out that the Otis County director's position became open when old lady Sinclair died. I was ready to leave Columbia, where I worked as assistant director. I knew I could never move into the director's position there, the competition was too great.

"I really didn't know that Sonny Boy and his family were living in Otis. When I got the offer and came to look the town over, I ran into him at the cleaners. I told him what happened and I said that I'd decline the position. He insisted that I take the job. He told me that he never revealed Brenda's real mother to his wife, and that Brenda had been adopted by Tootsie and was told that she was her real mother. He jokingly told me that if anything ever happened to him and Tootsie, it would be my duty to take care of *our* little girl.

"Four years later, when Sonny Boy died and left Tootsie and Brenda almost penniless, it was easy for me to believe that the good Lord meant for me to be near the child, for at least one of her birth parents to look after her and see that she'd be okay. Brenda took to me right off. I hadn't tried to develop a friendship with her until after Sonny Boy died," Hattie added, her voice cracking. "But right afterward, while Tootsie was so broken up over Sonny Boy's dying, I asked her if she'd mind if I gave Brenda some special attention. Tootsie gladly accepted.

"Maybe it was because of me that Brenda was so judgmental about others. I didn't want her to fall into the trap I'd fallen into, to make the same mistakes." Hattie closed her eyes, then opened them. "Brenda was such a good-hearted little girl, Candi. I'm not saying this to make myself feel better. This is not about me. It was my decision to give her up, my decision to let Sonny Boy let her believe that Tootsie was her real mother. I suppose I will always beat myself up about that, but that's not what's important right now!"

Silence.

"All week long I've been trying to figure out not only who killed my daughter but whether my constant badgering her about doing the right thing, no matter who it hurt, was the reason she was murdered!"

Mama put her arms around her boss and hugged her. Brenda Long had exposed others' secrets, but she had gone to her grave not knowing a very important one of her own.

CHAPTER

FIFTEEN

At six the next morning when I got up, I found my mother at the kitchen table, the notebook she'd been using to jot down notes she'd learned about Brenda was opened in front of her. The smell of southern butter pecan, my current favorite flavored coffee, permeated the whole house.

"You've been sitting here all night?" I teased.

Mama looked up. A small wrinkle was on her forehead. "It seems like it," she admitted.

"Slept badly, did you?"

"Yes," she told me. "Bad dreams."

"I know the feeling," I told her as I poured my first cup of coffee. "Monsters invaded my slumber too."

"Brenda's been dead a week. My intuition tells me that everything I need to know is right before me." Mama sounded exasperated. "It's just that I can't see it."

"Can't see the forest for the trees, huh?"

"What?"

"You know the old saying: a person can't see the forest for the trees because they're too close to the action."

"I could be too close to things," she said softly. "Perhaps I'm looking at each piece of the puzzle instead of the whole picture."

My father joined us. He drank a cup of coffee, then proceeded to go outside and fool around with Midnight. He, like me, had no doubts that this Saturday morning breakfast was going to be special because Cliff was expected.

At eight-thirty, Cliff arrived. He jumped out of his car, hugged and kissed me, then said, "Let's eat."

And we did just that. We had not only a great breakfast but we had a leisurely one. My father talked about a reunion his buddies were planning at the end of the month. Cliff told us a few stories of nasty divorces that kept him going back and forth like a seesaw. Mama didn't say much but she didn't hurry us—I got the impression that she enjoyed the relaxed atmosphere.

After breakfast, I tried to get Cliff to go for a drive but he refused. "The only effort I want to exert is to lie on your mother's couch and work my eyelids up and down."

"You're not going to spend the weekend sleeping and eating!" I declared.

"Try me."

"No way," I told him. "Let's play rummy."

"I can do that," he said. "If I can play while lying down on the couch in the family room."

I helped Mama with the dishes while Cliff and my father retreated to the family room. "What's your plans?" I asked Mama while cleaning off the table.

"I'm going to the Wesmart."

"Shopping?"

"Not exactly. Something is bothering me about that night Brenda was dropped off at the store, it's like a pull that I can't explain. Perhaps if I go sit in the parking lot, it'll come to me," she said, introspectively.

With my folks out of the house, Cliff and I had time to talk. And talk we did. All kinds of subjects were broached. Every subject that is, except one: our marriage.

"Simone," Cliff told me, "I really missed you this week. Especially when I went to your apartment to water your plants. It was almost like the world was out of sorts, out of place. Do you know what I mean?"

"I hope I do," I confessed.

"Seriously," he continued. "For the first time since we've been seeing each other my not being able to see you made my world feel like it was on a slant."

"Is that good or bad?"

"You think I'm jiving, don't you?"

"I think you're a very sweet man and I love you for it."

"Do you?" he asked.

"Of course I do."

"Love me now, but—"

"But, what?"

"Will you get tired of that love?"

"How can you get tired of loving somebody?"

"People get tired," Cliff said. "Tired, angry, and bitter. Gil Walters, one of the lawyers in the firm, was found guilty last week of assaulting his wife. They were going through a divorce and Gil became so angry that he went to her job and started beating her up. Not only did he have to pay a fine but he is also facing disciplinary action from the Georgia Commission on Lawyer Conduct. When Gil told me that his wife had filed for the divorce, all I could think of was how happy they both looked on their wedding day, how they vowed to be together until death."

"You're afraid of that happening to you?" I asked.

"You and me, we're good for each other. I mean, things are right with us the way things are now, don't you think?"

"I feel that we're a couple," I agreed.

"Yeah, but can we keep that togetherness?"

"My parents have kept it."

"I know," Cliff said. "Every time I get so caught up in a nasty divorce, I think about your parents and a measure of my faith in the institution of marriage is restored."

"You never told me about your parents," I said, thinking that the few times Cliff mentioned anybody in his family was when he was joking about some silly trait or idiosyncrasy.

"The truth is, I don't know much about my parents, Simone. My father and mother are both lawyers, defense lawyers. They worked hard with long hours. I had sitters, until I was able to go to school."

"I'd like to meet your parents."

"I'd like you to meet them too, but—" He hesitated.

"But, what?"

"I don't know," he admitted. "Truth is, Simone, I know your mother better than I do my own."

"Cliff," I said, "are you afraid that your mother won't like me?"

Cliff looked confused. "I don't know what my mother likes. On the few occasions I call home, she is cordial, but the truth is, I get the feeling that if I never called, she wouldn't mind."

I started to say something else when I heard the key in the door. My father yelled, "I'm home," like he wanted to make sure we knew he was in the house before he burst into the family room and saw me and Cliff doing something that would embarrass him.

"We know!" I hollered back reassuringly.

"Don't sound so disappointed," Daddy replied as he joined us.

"I'm not disappointed."

"I've decided that you two have had enough of this being together. Candi told me to give you two some time since you haven't really seen each other all week.

I've given you"—he looked at his watch—"four hours. Enough. Cliff, my boy, I have just pulled together two of the best bid-whisk players this county has living in it! Coal and Buddy will be here in a half hour. The cold beer, the peanuts, and potato chips are in the backseat of my car. We're half an hour away from throwing down with some *serious* card players."

Cliff jumped up from the sofa like he was a jackrabbit. "I'll get the food from your car!"

"I'm getting the card table and chairs. Simone," my father ordered, "move that chair back so that we'll have a little more space."

Needless to say, that was the end of my conversation with Cliff.

Watching four grown men act like little boys bickering over a deck of cards just isn't my idea of a fun Saturday afternoon. I tried to watch television, but that didn't work.

Fortunately, Mama came back home shortly after the game started.

"Boy, am I glad to see you," I told her. "Did a lightbulb go off in your head to help you understand what was bugging you about Wesmart?"

"No," Mama answered after letting out a deep thoughtful breath, "but I did learn something very interesting about the relationship between Clyde and Brenda!"

CHAPTER
SIXTEEN

"Okay," I said once my mother and I had been seated at the kitchen table. "Tell me all about what you've learned."

"I told you that I was going to Wesmart," she began. "Well, instead of taking the direct route through town, I decided to take the long way so that I could swing by Tootsie's house. The block before I got to Tootsie I saw Clyde with that boy Stone Washington. I was about to circle the block when Clyde said good-bye and jumped on his motorcycle. On an impulse, I followed him."

"And?" I asked in anticipation.

"He drove to where Brenda's body had been found. I watched him for a second, then I decided to approach him. When he spotted me, he hopped on his bike and sped off." Mama opened her hand and showed me a crumpled paper hospital ID bracelet with the name Brenda Long written on it. "Clyde slipped his hand in his pocket. When he pulled it out, he dropped this. When I saw it fall, I didn't think much of it but once he'd gone and I walked over to where he was standing, I saw what it was and I picked it up.

"So, Simone, instead of going to Wesmart, I decided to go to the hospital. Fortunately, Gertrude was on duty. Now, Simone, what I'm about to say can cost Gertrude her job. I feel a bit guilty that Gertrude went to this length, but I can't say I'm sorry she found out what I'm about to tell you."

"You don't have to tell me that!" I said anxiously.

"Gertrude got one of the clerks in the hospital's record room to check Brenda's hospital record. A year ago, Brenda had a miscarriage. She had an outpatient D and C."

I couldn't believe what Mama was saying. "You're not talking about the same Brenda Long that your boss told us was a saint?" I asked, disbelieving.

"The same," Mama told me. "But that's not the whole story. Brenda's record indicated that Clyde Hicks gave a pint of blood in her behalf."

"Are you trying to tell me that Brenda and Clyde had a thing for each other?" I snapped my fingers. "Wait a minute, that might have been what Dolly was alluding to when she told us that Clyde cared for Brenda."

"I was thinking the same thing," Mama con-

cluded. "Remember, too, Stella told us that Brenda
had gotten two kinds of letters from Clyde. The first
were threatening but there were others in which he
apologized. I wonder whether or not Tootsie knew
of Brenda's dilemma?"

"If she did, I'll give you ten to one she'll deny it."

Mama shrugged. "You're right. Whatever reason
she's got for pretending she doesn't know things
about Brenda is beyond me. But that's another can
of worms." My mother took a deep breath, and although she didn't say anything more, I could see
her struggling to find answers that made sense.

Our Sunday dinner was beef tenderloin steaks,
potato salad, succotash, mustard greens, buttery
rolls, and coconut cream pie. The centerpiece
Mama had picked up from the florist was a full bouquet of pink and white carnations.

As soon as we helped clean the kitchen, Cliff and
I headed back to Atlanta. We were driving separate
cars so we couldn't talk. I spent the drive contem-
plating the visit of Naomi Flowers, the college classmate I hardly remembered. The more I thought
about picking her up from the airport the next day,
the more my sixth sense warned that the experience
was going to be a nightmare. My feelings were on
target. Never will that woman come near me
again—it was like living with a Tasmanian devil.

Now, don't get me wrong, I'm not a neatnik. But

there has to be a measure of order in a one-bedroom apartment just to get around in it. You can't imagine the chaos that Naomi brought to my little place on Monday evening when she loaded it with three full-sized suitcases. The woman must have packed every piece of clothing she owned. When she opened each one and pulled out clothes, she threw them into every corner of the place.

My apartment was assassinated by the time Naomi headed for my refrigerator. Miss Thang opened the refrigerator door and decided that I needed groceries. She insisted that we go to the Kroger's she'd seen on our way into the complex.

The groceries cost me ninety-eight dollars. Two heads of lettuce, tomatoes, five different salad dressings, juices, lemons, olives, pickles, bananas, apples, Cokes, a three-tier chocolate layer cake, and twelve Hershey bars were just a few things that filled my shopping cart.

Oh, yeah! Did I mention the wine? She insisted on buying four bottles of a $7.99 chardonnay that she swore was as good as any she'd ever had.

Then my darling Naomi told me she wanted to go dancing. I had to work the next morning, work that had piled up after a week of so-called community service in Otis. She accepted that, but I was stuck with listening to the television all night.

Tuesday morning I was late for work. Naomi took a shower that lasted at least an hour. An hour before I could get into *my* bathroom. She tried on five or six outfits, got my opinion on each, only to disregard it.

Breakfast was juice, lettuce, tomato, and toast. She swore it's the best way to start the day.

When I dropped Naomi off at the Hilton downtown I fantasized that I wouldn't pick her up after I got off from work. Instead, I'd let her wander around the city for the remainder of her visit, then let her figure out how to get back to Kansas City on her own. After I was sure she was out of Atlanta, I'd pack up her things and UPS them to her.

The idea was pleasing but I knew I'd never be able to pull it off. Reality brought depression again, so I called Mama to cry on her shoulder, only to learn that things were almost as bad for her. Hattie Russell was challenging, criticizing, and complaining that she wasn't doing her job correctly at the agency. Why was I not surprised? My original apprehension had been justified. Hattie's grief for Brenda had spilled over into her professional role. Mama was feeling the fallout at work from her boss. And she'd continue to feel the heat until Brenda's killer was locked up.

Despite my mother's problem, she listened to me and comforted me by promising to cook something special when Naomi left Atlanta to return to Kansas City.

After I hung up with Mama, I tried to think of someplace to take Naomi after work that would wear her out so that I could get a good night's sleep.

I took her to the Underground. It's a popular tourist spot, with shops and places to eat.

Although Naomi had eaten fifty dollars' worth of food at the restaurant in the Underground, when we got back to the apartment, she raided the refrigerator, turned on the television, grabbed herself a handful of Hershey bars, and burrowed in for the night.

Wednesday morning my guest announced she needed a man. "Any man," she told me. "I'm desperate. There ain't no way I can go back to Kansas City and tell my friends I didn't have a good time with an Atlanta brother!"

Now, I wasn't about to put Miss Thang onto Cliff. Not that I felt threatened by her. It was just that I was in love with the guy, and my conscience wouldn't let me put something like Naomi Flowers on any man I had the least amount of respect for. I tried to come up with somebody who owed me, big-time.

So I called Yasmine, my best girlfriend. She and I put our heads together. She finally came up with a co-worker's name. Deshan, according to Yasmine, had just been dumped by his lady because of his infamous playing around. It took less than an hour for Yasmine to hook things up for Naomi with Deshan.

Deshan picked Naomi up from my apartment at eight. He brought her back at four the next morning.

Thursday morning, three hours after she got home, the girl was back in the shower. Then she packed. She had a 9:30 A.M. flight out of Hartsfield. No sooner had I waved her good-bye as she boarded her plane than I rushed to the telephone and called Shirley, the office manager.

"I'm sick," I told her, trying to sound even more exhausted than I felt. "Migraine headache."

"I didn't know you suffered with migraines," Shirley replied suspiciously.

"It's blinding," I lied. "I can hardly see."

"What's all that background noise?"

"Television," I said, having forgotten that my being at the noisy airport might make her wonder how sick I could be. "I'll call you if I feel better." I hastily hung up the phone and headed for my apartment, where I took a hot shower, rubbed my feet with Vaseline, put on pajamas and a pair of socks, and fell into my bed.

Thursday evening Mama called to say that as she was jotting things in her notebook she remembered Hattie mentioning that she'd seen Victor with Tootsie after Stella told us he'd left town. Mama made it a point to check further and she discovered that the man we'd seen leave Tootsie's house with her was Victor Powell.

"Let me know what else you find out," I told my mother. "I won't be coming back to Otis for a few more weeks, but I'd like to know how things are progressing."

That was the plan, that is, until I got another call from Mama around five o'clock the next evening.

There was a deep sadness in her voice. "This afternoon old man Elliott left a basket of tomatoes on the front porch. When I took the tomatoes out to wash them, I found a small plastic bag with the word 'viper' written on it at the bottom of the basket.

"I tried to call Elliott to ask him about the bag, but he didn't answer his phone. After supper, I drove to his house."

Mama paused. "As I pulled up in his driveway, I spotted Clyde Hicks pulling away on a motorcycle. I tried to get him to stop, but he ignored me. Simone, I found Elliott's body in his vegetable garden. He'd been strangled, and his tongue was slit in two."

CHAPTER
SEVENTEEN

Cliff and I left Atlanta before six o'clock the next morning.

When we walked in the door, my heart sank. Mama's expression was tinged with uncertainty. A thin line formed around her mouth. I searched my memory, then just put my arms around her trying to remember the last time I'd seen her like this.

"Simone, I've made a big mistake," Mama told me like she was apologizing. "I mean, I found those plastic bags, hard evidence that it was drugs that tied Brenda, Kitty, and Elliott's deaths together. Because of Lew Hunter's attitude, I refused to see it. That's why I kept looking at pieces of information and wasn't able to put them into any pattern. I let my personal feelings taint my perspective. Yesterday, after I'd called you, I got into my car and began to drive around town to take a closer look at Otis's teenagers. For a while all I could see were healthy, ordinary kids. Then I began to see that a few of our young people did look somewhat haggard, bony, almost like they were wasting away. I ran into one of my co-worker's daughters, Mary Jo Palmer. Mary was always a pretty girl, one who was particular about her appearance. Something about her had changed, she was noticeably thin, I could see all the veins in her arms and legs. Her clothes hung on her like she was a lamppost, her nails had been bitten off. I tried to talk to her, but she didn't seem interested in anything I had to say. Her pupils were dilated and the few words I got her to say were slurred. The facts were staring me in the face. Lew Hunter was right, I was being naive."

"Are you saying that you no longer think Clyde had anything to do with the murders?" I asked.

"Clyde had a thing for Brenda and he must have known Kitty Sharp, but, other than being near each victim before they died, I don't know of anything that ties him to the drugs."

"Don't let it all overwhelm you, you've figured out things like this before."

"There's a lot of information to digest and I've been up most of the night trying to put it all in context with somebody selling drugs on the high school campus. I've written down every word I can remember they've said. So far, my efforts have proven useless. I just can't come up with anything except—"

"What?"

"These things didn't start to happen until Ray Raisin moved back to Otis, which makes me wonder whether or not he's Otis's enterprising drug dealer. Agatha knows something about Ray, something that suggests that the man isn't as squeaky clean as he appears. What Agatha knows may be the missing piece that will bring everything else we've learned into perspective."

"I tried to get her to tell me about him, but she refused," I reminded Mama.

"Perhaps after I tell Agatha about Otis's drug problem and what it's doing to our young people, she'll share her secret with us!"

Mama told me that she had an appointment with Lew and Abe at one o'clock and she wanted to visit Agatha before she talked to them. I spoke with Cliff, told him of our plans. He and my father had already decided to team up with Coal and a few other of my father's cronies for a day of playing cards and drinking beer. Satisfied that they'd be at it until the wee hours of the morning, I gave him a kiss and waved good-bye as Mama and I drove away.

Twenty-five minutes later, we were seated in Agatha's front room and my mother had asked about Ray Raisin.

"Agatha, this is not a matter of gossip—this is a matter of life and death."

Agatha took a deep breath. "Everybody thinks that Ray Raisin is a fine, successful man. There's no use digging up something about him that has been put to rest all these years."

"Under different circumstances, I'd agree with you," Mama told her. "But a young girl is dead along with two other people, and drugs have infiltrated our high school. And it all happened since Ray Raisin moved back home to Otis. It's possible that he has more to do with what's going on than meets the eye. If you know something that can help, I need to know it. The reason I came to you is that it's clear that you're not prejudiced by his appearance. You don't see Ray as a prince in shining armor the way that Carrie, Sarah, and Annie Mae do."

"That's 'cause Carrie, Sarah, and Annie Mae don't know Ray the way I do," Agatha said.

"Tell us," Mama urged.

Agatha glanced at Mama, then looked down at her lap. She began to move her hands over her apron, as if she was trying to smooth invisible wrinkles out of it. "Ray and I went to school together. Back then, there were only eight of us in the classroom. Four girls, four boys. Only eight children who didn't have to work in the cotton fields, eight children whose parents made enough to feed them, to pay a teacher and send them to school.

"Our teacher, Hazel Putnam, got a letter from the Methodist church headquarters in Columbia. The church had collected enough money to send one child to high school, maybe on to college. It was Miss Putnam's charge to pick which one of us would be given the opportunity."

"Hazel Putnam selected Ray Raisin and you've never forgiven him?" I asked.

"No," Agatha said firmly. "Miss Putnam picked *me!* I was head and shoulders smarter than Ray and he knew it!"

"But—"

"I was picked to go to high school and to college," Agatha continued, "but Ray was so determined to get that chance that he paid one of the other boys to tell the teacher that I was womanish, that he had overheard me offering to do things with Ray that wasn't proper!"

"So the teacher decided to send Ray instead of you," I said.

Agatha nodded. "Things were different in my day. Morals didn't exist in shades of gray like they do today. Candi, you know people looked at morals as either right or wrong. The church had made it clear that chastity was a high priority in selecting the student. Ray, who put on the appearance of being holier-than-thou, wasn't the smartest but he presented himself as the more righteous. He got the chance I wanted—no, the chance I *deserved*. He stole my education, and the talk that he set out against me hung around my neck for years."

"Is that why you never married?"

Agatha didn't answer my question. "After Ray

was gone for six months, the other fella admitted to my father that Ray had pushed him up to lie, but it was too late. The lying Ray Raisin ended up a high-brow lawyer and I'm—"

"The smartest businesswoman this area has ever known," Mama said, finishing Agatha's sentence.

Agatha shrugged. "I used to sit on our front porch and wonder how far I could have gone if I had been given that chance. Truth is, I hate the way he's come back home acting like he wants me to believe he's sorry for what he did. Being so polite and nice, telling Sarah, Carrie, and Annie Mae that he wants to visit me. He must be crazy to think I would have forgotten what he'd done forty-five years ago!"

For a moment none of us spoke. "The sky would have been your limit," I finally said. "If you had gotten that scholarship it's no telling what you might have become."

Agatha's eyelids blinked, then she looked away. "What might have been doesn't matter now, does it? The fact is that it wasn't me that touched the sky, it was Ray Raisin. I guess I should be Christian-like and forgive him, but the truth is he never changed. I kept up with what was going on in his life. He's a liar, a good-for-nothing person who pretends that he got what he has straight-up like the good Lord meant him to have it. I've got an article from a New Jersey newspaper that shows Ray lost his license to practice law twenty years ago. One of Daddy's cousins sent it to me. She told me that Ray was involved in something illegal, that she had seen him and told him that she was going to send me the article out of the newspaper."

"Where is that article?" Mama asked.

Agatha got up and went into her room. When she returned her hands were empty, her mouth open. "It's gone!"

CHAPTER
EIGHTEEN

We spent an hour combing through Agatha's closet, which held boxes upon boxes of clothes she'd never live long enough to wear. According to Agatha, everything was accounted for except a large box where she kept family pictures, mementos, obituaries, graduation programs, wedding announcements, and newspaper clippings.

"Why would anybody steal pictures, things having special meaning to only you or your family?" I asked.

"It doesn't make sense," Mama replied. "Whoever came in here and took it must have known that you were spending a few days with us when you were ill."

"That could have been anybody in the county," I said, thinking of Annie Mae, Carrie, and Sarah. Once they got wind of Agatha's stay with us, it would be all over the county in a matter of hours.

Agatha didn't say anything, but she paced the floor, wringing her hands until I thought they'd blister. She was a smart and talented woman who'd spent her life preserving our family's heritage. Now that accomplishment had been taken away from her.

Anger flashed through me for what Ray Raisin had denied her. I had been born at a time when I could be spared such indignities. I could get as much or as little education as I chose. It was something I rarely thought about, but now outrage welled up inside of me and made me feel like I'd been personally attacked.

What happened next was totally unexpected and caught us all by surprise.

There was a knock on the door.

Ray Raisin stood on the porch, a large box in his hand, the one I surmised belonged to Agatha. His face was draped with disgrace, like it was painful for him to have come. "I'd like to return your box. It shames me that it's in my possession."

Agatha's eyes shot darts at him.

Mama took charge. "Come in."

Ray hesitated for a moment, then swept into the room. He sat on the sofa, put the box on the floor and stared at it, his hands clasped loosely in his lap.

The three of us stared back at him.

His gaze shifted to Agatha. "I owe you an apology—no, I owe you several apologies. You see, I came into your house uninvited and borrowed your box of mementos. I—"

"I hate you!" Agatha spat.

"You should hate me," he replied evenly.

A look of annoyance flashed across my mother's face. "Why in heaven's name did you break into Agatha's house?"

"I wanted a newspaper clipping, the one that reported I'd lost my license to practice law. I worked my butt off, but I made some bad decisions. Hell, I was young, without an inkling of how to handle myself in the city when I first got out of law school. I made a few bad choices. When things went bad, it took me years to clear up my legal problems, to overcome the scandals, but I did it. I got my license back and things got better. And when my poor wife died, I decided to give up my practice and come back home. I felt this was the one place on earth I could die in peace and everybody made me feel I'd made the right decision. Everybody except Agatha, that is. After she treated me the way she did at the community center, I was sure she'd show people the clipping and once again I'd be the center of rumors and gossip."

Mama's impatience intensified. "You're a lawyer, you know that's not a reason to break into Agatha's house."

Ray looked genuinely remorseful. "I didn't destroy the clipping. I intended to destroy it, intended to bring the box back. By the time I'd decided to return the things undisturbed, Agatha had come home."

Mama gave him a long look as if she was trying to decide whether or not to believe him. "Why did you bring the box back today?"

"I got a call an hour ago from Calvin Stokes."

"The lawyer?"

He nodded. "You know that my family owned quite a bit of land in the area at one time. Well, they lost it. Now the only property that's in the family is an acre and a house. Calvin told me that he owned twenty-five acres around the homestead and he was interested in selling it. He'd called Agatha and asked her whether she knew anybody interested in buying it. Agatha told him that the land had belonged to my family, that I was back home, and that I should be given the first offer to buy it back."

"It's only right," Agatha muttered.

"After Calvin and I spoke and I hung up the phone I realized that Agatha wasn't holding a grudge. I realized something else too. I finally realized how much I was indebted to her, how it was time to stop being afraid of not getting what I wanted. It was time for me to start giving something back to Agatha. This box is my first effort to do that."

Mama's look sent Ray Raisin the message that she understood that there are people who'll do you in and not care how much pain they inflict and that she considered him one of those people. "Since you seem to be in the mood to confess your sins, are you so low that you've been distributing drugs to the young people in this town?"

Ray jumped up like he'd been rammed in the rump with a poison dart. "Is that what you think of me?"

"That doesn't answer my question," Mama told him.

Now, I've said before that my mother's manner is usually warm, and gently persuasive. Not this time!

Ray stepped back, his eyes locked on my mother's. He seemed to start to say something, but decided against it. Instead, he asked, "Why would I do that?"

Agatha spoke, tears choking her words. "Because the good Lord took that law license away from you, to punish you for the way you schemed and lied to get it."

"I'll never be able to meet my Maker in peace because of that lie."

"If you lie once, you'll lie twice," Mama jabbed.

"I don't sell drugs to children!" Ray hollered.

"Do you own a black Jaguar?" Mama challenged.

"What?"

"You heard my question."

He scanned Mama's face, then broke off eye contact. "No, I don't own a black Jaguar, nor a red or white Jaguar. God, this is all so screwed up. I can't believe this is happening. I didn't mean for things to go this way."

Ray Raisin sounded like a self-indulgent teenager with no concern for dishonesty. In my head, I could see how a youthful Ray schemed to cheat my cousin out of her scholarship. I'd misjudged the man. Now he looked like a dressed-up common thief, the kind I'd seen many times in my work.

Mama's brow wrinkled. "What did you expect when you come in here acting like a remorseful soul? That Agatha would have the town give you a parade and put up welcome banners?"

"If Agatha wants to press charges against me for breaking in and stealing her box, she can do it. I'm prepared to pay the price for what I've done."

There it was again, the foolish and empty statement of an old man with a adolescent's sense of right and wrong.

"What you've done to Agatha is no small matter, but it only highlights your capacity to hurt others. As far as I'm concerned, you're not only capable of selling drugs to our children, but you could just as well have killed Brenda, Kitty, and poor old Elliott because they caught on to you!"

Something stirred inside my head, the notion that in my experience working with a defense lawyer and dealing with convicted murderers or drug dealers, Ray Raisin's personality didn't fit the profile. Still, a few days earlier I'd thought he was what I wanted my man to look like in his senior years—I could be wrong again.

He looked at Mama like he realized the force of her accusations. "The State Law Enforcement man is looking for a teenager. If it were me, I'd be looking for a kid that's almost scared to death."

He turned to Agatha. "I'm sorry, really sorry for

what I've done to you," he apologized. "I won't trouble you any longer."

Then he left.

"You want to report that he broke into your house and stole your box?" I asked Agatha.

She made a face and shook her head in disgust.

"Do you want us to check to see if everything is still in the box?"

"I . . . I can't right now. I'm sorry, but I can't—"

"You want us to go?" Mama asked.

"I'm sorry—"

"We understand," Mama reassured her. "I'll call you later."

"I . . . I'm sorry," Agatha repeated, and burst into tears.

CHAPTER

NINETEEN

"What do you think of Ray Raisin now?" I asked just before we pulled up in front of the sheriff's office.

"He's slick," Mama confessed.

"Afraid I don't see him as Otis's enterprising drug dealer."

"I don't know," Mama muttered, frustrated. "My theory seemed plausible a few hours ago."

"The more I think of Ray, the more I realize that he doesn't fit the profile of a drug dealer. When you take the nature of the crime, the circumstances surrounding when it happened and how it happened, and you look at the physical evidence, things like hair samples, nails, blood, fingerprints, and mix these elements together you'd have to conclude that Ray isn't the type of person we're looking for."

"You're trying to tell me you've looked at all those things with Ray in mind?"

"Of course not, but in my opinion, he fits the slicker profile whose main game is to get over on people."

"Ray is a thief and a liar in a business suit, I know that already."

"I mean that's about all he's good for. He's too conceited to go after anything outside of himself and, judging from his having been disbarred, he's not very good at what he does. If he had a drug ring going on, he'd have been caught by now."

"Are you saying that drug dealers aren't conceited?"

"That's not what I'm saying and you know it."

The look on my mother's face was a combination of worry and irritation. "I know what you're saying, Simone, and the truth is, I'm inclined to agree with you. Something is right in front of my face and I can't see it. Brenda had seen it, that's why she was killed. If only she had left us a clue, something that would point us in the right direction.

Lew Hunter was talking to the dispatcher when we arrived. After a cordial greeting, he escorted us into Abe's office. As we were being seated, I looked around the room. A cream-colored cinder-block wall directly behind Abe's large desk had a new bulletin board. Colored tacks and what I assumed were crime-scene pictures covered it.

Lew eased the door shut behind us. Abe was conspicuously missing but the room stank of cigarette smoke and ashtrays were spilling over with cigarette butts. Somehow, I felt he wasn't far away.

Lew looked tired. Not like he'd missed a night's sleep, but like he'd missed two weeks' sleep. "It looks like we're again talking about your discovery of a body," he said.

Mama threw him a look that said something was happening that she didn't understand. "I suppose you want to know the purpose of my visit to Elliott's last night?"

"Let's wait until Abe returns," he said. "He's just down the hall in the john."

I knew that Mama was all ready to explain that Elliott had left a basket of tomatoes and she went to his house to pay him for them, that she'd seen Clyde pull away on a motorcycle, that she'd tried to stop him, but he wouldn't stop. And I understood that what she really wanted was any new information that would help her in her own inquiry. But instead of a maneuvering conversation, there was silence.

Mama shifted in her seat. Her movement was slight, but I saw it.

Abe finally came into the room. He walked over to his desk, sat down and picked up a pack of Camels and stuck one in the corner of his mouth.

Lew took a book of matches out of his pocket, but Abe told him not to strike it. "Candi can't take the smoke.

"Ain't no use going over why you happened upon Elliott's body last night, Candi. Fact is, if you hadn't found him somebody else would have."

That sounded like the old Abe talking, I thought, the law officer that my mother had worked with many times before. I wanted to think he'd wrested control of the situation from Lew, but I didn't want to jump the gun too quickly.

He threw Lew a warning look. "I've spent some time talking to the head of the narcotics department at SLED and he agrees with me that we're a pretty close-knit town, that we believe in one hand washing the other. Now, I know that Lew here is used to dealing with drug dealers with their noses pierced, and long, nasty hair hanging halfway down their backs. Maybe he doesn't quite understand the way people around here think. I mean, I have to give him credit— he's found out some important things from his laboratory reports, things that got us heading in the right direction. But he's come to agree with me that to get information and names from our people, lab reports won't help. Folks around here talk to people they trust. I think a measure of confusion has come up because we didn't combine what we got from the crime lab with a good thinking person."

Mama's eyes suddenly had a glint in them. I suspected, like me, she was beginning to see that the tables had turned, that Abe had taken back the case, and that she once again was a part of his team.

Lew's mouth pulled down. "I suppose I should

tell you what we've learned from our lab reports. Fingerprints, hair, and skin samples found at the crime scene prove that Brenda and Kitty were killed by the same person. I'm sure once I get the lab report on Elliott, it'll be confirmed that he too was killed by that person."

"Something else, Candi," Abe added. "The person we're looking for has no prior criminal record. Nothing in the computers matched anything we've picked up on the fella."

"We know that the killer is a black male," Lew continued, "that he's between sixteen and twenty-one, and that he had some marijuana and drunk beer shortly before he killed."

"Now, don't think we're not going to talk with Clyde again," Abe assured Mama. "It's just that since Clyde's been locked up before, we know everything there is about him, and his blood and fingerprints just don't match. As a matter of fact, we haven't found anything at any of the crime scenes that points to Clyde being there."

"Am I right that Brenda told you the person she fingered was a high school student?" Mama asked Lew.

"Yeah," he answered, "and despite the murders, the young people refuse to give us an inkling as to who this fella is. We've appealed to them through their teachers, through their preachers, and through their parents, but nobody will say a word."

"Is there anything unusual about this kid, I mean

something that will help me pick him from the rest of the students?"

"Jewelry!" I blurted, thinking of the drug dealers I'd seen in Atlanta. "They wear lots of gold and diamonds—the real thing!"

My words hit Mama like a bolt of lightning. Something seemed to have just jumped out of the recesses of her brain. "That's it!" she said, standing.

"What?" I asked, trying to follow her line of thought.

"Abe, was Brenda wearing any jewelry when you found her body?"

Abe thumbed through the papers on his desk, frowning. After a few seconds of reading through them, he looked up at my mother. "There's no mention of jewelry being found on the body or anyplace around it."

Mama motioned me toward the door. "There's something I need to check out," she told Abe and Lew. "As soon as I'm sure I'm right, I'll call you!"

CHAPTER
TWENTY

Whatever clouds of confusion had existed in my mother's mind, the look in her eyes told me that it was beginning to clear. "Simone," she said, "now I know what's been eluding me. Do you remember the jewelry we saw on Brenda's dressing table the first time we visited Tootsie?"

"Yeah," I told her. "It was a class ring and a beautiful designer watch."

"It was a class ring with a diamond stone in it, a diamond just like the one I picked up from Kitty's living room. Now, do you remember my remarking how attractive Stella's class ring was."

"Yeah."

"Stella's ring looked exactly like the one we saw on Brenda's dressing table except that it had a cheaper stone in it. Remember when you first got your high school class ring, how you kept it on your finger all the time?"

"Of course," I answered, remembering how proud I was to wear my high school ring.

"Let's visit Stella. If she tells us that Brenda had her ring on the night she was dropped off near Wesmart that means the killer took it off and somehow got it back into Tootsie's house and into Brenda's room after he'd killed her."

A half hour later, when Stella opened her front door, we were greeted by the smell of burnt fried meat and by a young woman whose short hair stuck up on her head like Buckwheat's. She wore an oversized gray T-shirt that hung almost to her knees, so that it was hard to tell whether she wore anything under it. Stella's eyes were red and puffy.

Mama tried small talk. "It's good to find you at home on a Saturday afternoon. Most young people are out shopping, getting ready for a fun Saturday night."

Stella looked at Mama blankly, walked over to the table, picked up a king-size Milky Way, ripped open the wrapper, and took a large bite. Then she walked over to the window, turned her back to us, and finished off the candy bar.

"Stella, I guess you're wondering why we're here?"

She nodded. I could hear her lips smack, and I

could see the back of her head bob up and down like a ball that had grown stubby hair.

"I want to discuss something very important with you. Come sit down next to me," Mama suggested.

Stella turned. Her eyes fixed coldly on Mama. When she spoke, I couldn't help but wonder whether this was the same callous, defiant manner she adopted with her stepfather the morning she'd provoked him into slapping her. "I don't want to sit down. What am I supposed to have done now?"

Mama let out a breath. "Stella," she said as if she was making a confession, "I need you to help me."

"Do what?"

"I need to know something about the person who's selling drugs at the school."

Stella threw up her hands in disgust. "Is that what this is all about? Miss Candi, you might as well pack your bags and get out of town if you think I'm going to tell you, or anybody else for that matter, about what's going on at school!"

Uh-oh, I thought. *Mama should have tried a different approach.*

"What did I say to get you so upset?"

Stella's jaw tightened. Mama's words might as well have been a red flag waving in front of her nostrils. "I'm sick and tired of people asking questions. Everything was going fine until Brenda decided that she was going to be holier-than-thou. Now a day doesn't go by that our teachers aren't on our backs. When I get home from school, Mama threatens to throw me out of the house if she just *thinks* I'm using drugs. And on Sundays, our preacher beat us over the head with sermons about the evil among us. Do you know, that policeman from Columbia has even got him passing out paper during Sunday school so that if the Lord moves us, we'll write down the name of one of our friends? What he doesn't know is that Brenda started something, then went off and got herself killed. Nobody, including me, is about to make the same mistake. Fact is, I don't care what another kid is doing as long as he doesn't mess with me."

"I suppose I should have realized how hard all of this has been on you kids." Empathy flashed in Mama's eyes.

But Stella continued lashing out. "What's with these overprotective, self-righteous grown-up speeches on what's wrong and what's right? I bet when you were a teenager you did everything you wanted to do. Now that you're old, and you can't have any fun, you've all of a sudden decided that anything that's the least bit fun is wrong!"

"I have to admit I did things my mother probably wouldn't have liked."

"And I bet when your mother got on your back to get you to squeal, you never told on your friends, did you?"

This was not my conversation, but truth is, I understood Stella's youthful rationale. The first rule to getting along with your peers is that you can't be a squealer. It's a sign of weakness, a character flaw that marks you for life. I remember a young girl named Trish who ran in my high school circle. Trish used to tell everything she knew and we avoided her like the plague. As a matter of fact, we used to tease her that the three fastest means of communication were telegraph, telephone, and teleTrish. Trish became a surgeon, a competent and extremely capable woman, but no matter how accomplished the adult Trish is, whenever we remember her we always refer to her as the class stool pigeon.

Stella might not have known Trish, but it was clear that she understood the consequences she'd have to endure if it were known that she had told an adult something about one of her classmates.

Mama didn't seem to pay any attention to Stella's reluctance. "Three people have been killed. Three innocent lives snuffed out."

"I ain't had nothing to do with that."

Mama got up, walked over to Stella, and touched her arm. Stella twitched as though she was going to jump. "I need your help," Mama said. "I need you to remember something very important, something that can bring an end to these terrible things that's been happening."

Stella continued to say nothing.

"Tell me," Mama continued, "do you remember whether or not Brenda wore her class ring and her watch that last Thursday afternoon she came to your house?"

Stella's look was steady but slightly warmer. "What?" she asked like she couldn't believe what Mama wanted to know. "She had on her Anne Klein watch and her ring, which is just like mine except for the diamond."

Mama opened her purse and took out a piece of tissue paper. She opened it to reveal the small diamond. "Let me see your ring again," she asked.

Stella held up her ring finger. The diamond was the same exact size as the stone centered in Stella's ring.

Stella looked surprised, almost dumbfounded. "Did that come from Brenda's ring?" she asked.

When Mama shook her head, Stella let out a sigh of relief. "Brenda loved that ring. She'd roll over in her grave if she thought something had happened to it."

"Do you know if any other student had a class ring exactly like the one Brenda had?" Mama asked.

For the seconds of quietness, it was almost as if Stella understood what Mama was asking and she was reluctant to answer. Then the words slipped from Stella's lips. "Brenda and Stone Washington were the only two students who ordered that ring with the diamond center. I wanted one like theirs but my mother wouldn't get the money from Victor to buy it for me."

CHAPTER
TWENTY-ONE

When we walked out of Stella's house, Mama had an intense look on her face. "Simone, do you realize what we've just learned? Stone Washington. Let me think about him." She snapped her fingers, her eyes flashed with insight. "I saw Stone near the Wesmart the night Brenda was killed. It must have been sometime between seven-forty-five and eight because I was home at eight o'clock. I'd picked up a bouquet from the florist that's next door to Wesmart. Stone was driving his mama's old man's white Mercedes. I didn't think much of it at the time although I should have realized it when Abe mentioned that a woman saw Brenda getting into an expensive light-colored car around seven-fifty-five."

"Was Stone Washington that handsome teenager

who slipped through Tootsie's front door the first time we visited her?" I asked.

Mama nodded. "Yes, of course. He was the one who brought clothes to the community center around the time Sarah, Annie Mae, and Carrie arrived and at that time he told us that Tootsie sent the bag. If Tootsie sent him to Brenda's room to get the bag, it would have been easy for him to put the ring and watch on Brenda's dressing table."

"Tootsie probably considered Stone as one of Brenda's friends, although she seemed at a loss to remember him when you asked about her daughter's friends."

"Sabrina Miley did tell us she'd heard that Brenda had a friend who was in trouble and she didn't have the sense to try to help him." She hesitated. "Now, let me see. Stone killed Brenda because she learned he was selling drugs and she wanted him to tell her the name of the person who was supplying him the stuff. He killed Kitty Sharp because she was the one who told Brenda what he was doing."

"Why kill poor old man Elliott?" I asked.

"Elliott talked a lot about the women who bought his vegetables. Come to think of it, I remember he mentioned that Stone was hanging around Tootsie's house a lot even though the woman's daughter was dead. And, of course there is the plastic bag I found in the basket of tomatoes. Who knows, Stone might have seen Elliott pick it up."

"Okay," I said, convinced. "Where to now?"

"Let's find Stone to see if his class ring is missing a diamond," she said introspectively.

I stopped at a gas station and filled my tank. Our trip was on the other side of the county, a few miles from Masonville, not far from where Brenda's body was found.

Mama opened her purse and began digging into it again.

"What are you looking for this time?" I asked.

"That picture that fell out of Brenda's books when Dolly gave them to us. It was a picture of Stone and two other boys in the Hot Chocolate Café." Once she had the small photo, she looked at it, then back at me. "Let's check this place out first," she told me. "Maybe we can catch up with Stone without having to go to his house."

We headed for the Hot Chocolate Café, a place where Mama told me most of the teenagers hung out. On one side of the columns was a large empty space. I imagined that was where the kids danced. On the other side was a pool table, and a few tables and chairs. Two or three signs stated No Alcohol Served. I don't know whether my mother heard me snicker as I thought of my own high school experience. A teenager could get a shot of whiskey at places like this if she said the right words to the right person.

Several boys were playing cards at two of the tables. They were laughing, and having a lot of fun.

A woman in her early fifties was sweeping the floor.

Mama addressed the woman. "Hello, Gladys."

"Hi you, Candi?"

"Very well, thank you. Gladys, I'm looking for Stone Washington. Have you seen him today? I'd like to talk to him."

The boys at the table stopped laughing and looked up, then, in a more quiet and serious mood, they went back to their game.

"You didn't pass him? He left two minutes ago," Gladys told Mama.

Mama shook her head. "Did he say where he was going?"

"Any of you boys remember where Stone say he was heading?" Gladys yelled.

"Home," one of the boys said, without bothering to look up at us again.

We went back to my Honda and headed in the direction Mama told me Stone lived. This section of town was owned by one of Otis's well-to-do citizens who, in the past few years, decided to build small wood-framed houses and then rent them out. Stone and his mother lived near the junction that cuts off into a two-lane highway toward Columbia. When we pulled into his front yard, the smell of pork chops scented the air.

I sat in the car and left the engine idling while Mama knocked on the door. A woman in her forties with dark eyes, shoulder-length unpermed hair that she wore in a ponytail, a pair of black-rimmed glasses, and an orange dress answered the door. "Miss Candi," the woman greeted my mother.

"It's good to see you, Lizzie."

"This is sure a surprise. What brings you here?"

By this time I'd joined Mama on Lizzie's front porch. Before Mama had a chance to tell her what she wanted, the phone rang.

Lizzie beckoned us inside. "Come on in." She ducked back into the house. We eased in the front door into a neatly furnished living room and sat on the couch. Directly opposite the couch was an open door that showed us a small bedroom. The bedroom wasn't very big, maybe twelve feet by ten. The bed was unmade. A large TV sat on a stand. You'd think a tornado had touched down in the room, the way the clothes were thrown around. I couldn't help but think of Naomi and how glad I was when I put her on the plane back to Kansas City.

"Now, that's a typical teenager's room," I told Mama.

"It's quite different from Brenda's room, isn't it?" she said.

"Tootsie told us she cleaned the room, remember?"

Mama nodded, a thoughtful look in her eyes.

When Lizzie came back into the room, a sour expression was on her face. "My old man is too sickening sometimes. Wants me to run over there just 'cause he's got a headache. Mind you, I can have pain from my head to my toe and he doesn't think much of it. But let him hurt in one spot and I'm supposed to drop everything and go see about him."

"We're not going to stay long," Mama assured her.

"Don't matter how long you stay, 'cause I ain't going over there until I get good and ready."

"We were looking for your son."

"Stone ain't done nothing to you, has he?"

"No, no. I just wanted to talk to him."

"He ain't much for conversation of late. I ain't had two words out of that boy for the past few weeks."

"Do you have any idea where I might find him now?"

"At his old lady's house," Lizzie said.

"Stone has a girlfriend?"

Lizzie had a wary look in her eyes, like she wasn't quite sure how she should tell us what was on her mind. "I'm Stone's mother and I tried to raise him right. Ask anybody around town, and they'd tell you I tried to teach him right from wrong. But when a boy gets a certain age, he won't let his mother tell him what to do no more. That's when his manhood starts calling, and that's a dangerous time—he's apt to get caught up in things that might not be fitting."

Mama nodded, like she understood perfectly.

"I wanted Stone to go with girls his own age," Lizzie continued. "Girls like him who don't know much about life. He said they were too young, they couldn't teach him anything.

"Candi, you mean to tell me that you hadn't heard that Stone's been going with Sonny Boy's wife for over a year now?"

The shock on Mama's face was clear; she shook her head mutely.

"I guess that's because people were thinking he was hanging around that place because he was seeing Tootsie's daughter. Tootsie buys him high-priced clothes, gold jewelry. Come over here and take a look in his room, you'll see what I'm talking about."

We followed Lizzie into the cluttered bedroom. Sure enough, the clothes we'd seen from where we were sitting on the couch weren't cheap. We saw gold chains and bracelets. More important, we saw a class ring. It was conspicuously placed on top of the nightstand, its oval diamond no longer in its setting. Alongside the ring were also a few twenty-dollar bills. Sticking out from under the bed was a shoe box full of little plastic bags with the word "viper" written on them.

Mama and I threw each other a look.

"I don't know where Tootsie gets so much money

from," Lizzie continued, "but she doesn't mind giving it to Stone. She even bought him a high-priced car and lets him keep it locked up in her garage." Lizzie gave us a nasty little grin. "I've told my old man more than once that whatever my boy is doing for that old woman, she sure feels like it's worth a lot of money."

"I really need to talk to Stone," Mama said, ignoring Lizzie's remark.

Lizzie rubbed her forehead wearily. "Stone used to come home sometimes but since Tootsie's daughter got killed, I hardly see him. If you want to get ahold of my boy, Tootsie is the woman to go see."

CHAPTER
TWENTY-TWO

Tootsie Long was a pretty woman, I've already told you that. But her beauty was that of a woman, a full-grown woman. Nothing in her manner would've made you suspect that she had a thing for a teenage boy.

The idea of a grown woman sleeping with a teenager brought back the memory of a situation I'd known. One of the boys in my high school class, Kenny Press, was sleeping with a grown woman and she controlled his every move. She wouldn't let poor Kenny go to any of the events that we went to because she was scared that he'd start talking to a girl his own age. When Kenny's teenage niece came to visit his family, the woman made him stay at her house. She claimed the girl was really Kenny's girlfriend. The whole thing got so out of hand that his family sent

Kenny away to another state just to break the hold this woman had on the poor boy.

We were back in my Honda, trying to get a fix on the situation. I looked at Mama, who stared out of the window toward the house. "I was suspicious of Tootsie the night she and Hattie came to the house," she muttered. "Something struck me as odd about the relationship she had with her daughter."

"Now that we know what's going on between her and Stone, don't you think it's time to call in the cavalry—time to give Abe and Lew everything we've learned?"

A flash of irritation crossed her face. "No," she answered quickly, "not yet!"

I didn't understand Mama's reluctance. "We know that only two students had the class ring with a diamond setting. We know Brenda's ring is intact because we saw it, and we know that Stone's ring is missing its stone, a stone you *shouldn't* have picked up from Kitty Sharp's living room. That's enough for Abe and Lew to work through the details of the murders," I told her. "What more is there for us to do?"

Mama's manner was *very* brisk. "Simone, listen. I've already told you that something was stirring in the back of my mind, my instinct was prodding me." Mama shifted impatiently. "That same instinct is screaming that with a little more effort we can get evidence that will put both a killer and a drug dealer behind bars for a long, long time. This time, I'm going to listen to it!"

"Stone Washington is the killer," I said.

"But we don't know who supplies him with the drugs."

"Tootsie Long," I contended.

"We can't prove that."

"Abe is now in charge of the case," I continued. "Let's talk it over with him."

"No. We can't be sure he won't let Lew Hunter take things over again."

I was unconvinced and Mama knew it but her eyes were focused on mine and I could see that her mental gears were working.

I took a deep breath. "Let's talk this out."

She cleared her throat and slipped her little notebook from her purse. "Okay, we've learned that Tootsie and Stone are lovers."

"That may be why Tootsie was so evasive when we asked about Brenda's friends."

"And why she was anxious to learn whether or not Lew Hunter was looking for a black Jaguar."

"The expensive car that had been hidden in her garage, the one Stone's mother told us Tootsie Long had bought for her son."

"What irritates me," she said, "is that I should have known, from the look of Tootsie's house with its stylish furniture, that she had a pretty good income."

"An income without a job should have been a red flag," I added.

"And then there was what Sabrina Miley had told

us. I should have paid more attention to her comment that she had a friend who'd seen Tootsie with a lot of money."

"Questionable money," I said.

After that, Mama was quiet for a moment. Finally, I glanced at my watch. The afternoon had turned into early evening. I understood what she wanted. It was more than turning Stone over to Abe and Lew. Mama wanted to nail Tootsie Long, the woman who while wearing a mask of innocence was ravaging Otis's young people with drugs. "What happens now?" I asked.

Mama closed her notebook and slipped it back into her purse. "Let's go to Tootsie's house. Stone doesn't know that we're on to him but if we drop the right hints to Tootsie, she'll let him know and he'll no doubt get in touch with us. I'll make sure Tootsie understands that we need to talk to Stone about both Brenda's death and the drugs that are being sold on the school campus. That should get us some action. If this plan doesn't work, I'll call Lew and Abe first thing tomorrow morning and tell them everything we've learned. They can handle it after that."

The look in my eyes must have told Mama that I wasn't so sure our next move was a wise one because she reached over and patted my hands. "We'll be all right," she assured me. "I don't think Stone or Tootsie would be so brazen as to try to kill us tonight."

Mama, who is usually right, was totally wrong on this assessment.

Half an hour later, Mama told Tootsie that she wanted her to give Stone the message that she wanted to talk to him. Tootsie's eyebrows rose. "Why do you want to talk with Stone?"

"I saw Stone near the Wesmart the night Brenda was murdered," Mama replied. "He was driving Lizzie's old man's car, a white Mercedes. Abe told me that he talked to a woman who saw Brenda get into an expensive light-colored car around seven-fifty-five."

Tootsie's eyes opened in surprise. "You never mentioned this to me before now."

"That's because I had forgotten it," Mama told her. "Until just a few minutes ago, I didn't remember seeing Stone driving Bo Pete's white Mercedes that night."

By the time Mama had finished those words, the small plastic bag with the word "viper" written on it, the one she'd just gotten from Stone's bedroom, had slipped from her purse. Like the seductive lure at the end of a fishhook, it fell to the floor in front of Tootsie's chair. I watched to see how she'd react.

Tootsie looked at the bag, then back up at my mother, and said, "Stone is a fine young man, you know. He helps me out quite a bit around this place."

Mama leaned forward and slowly picked up the bag.

She slipped it into her purse and snapped it shut. "I understand he spends a great deal of time visiting you."

The look in Tootsie's eyes told me that my mother had just reeled in a drug dealer. "Stone sees to it that the yard is cut, the car is serviced, things like that. I hope you haven't been listening to the twisted talk of people who ain't got nothing to do but gossip. I mean, why shouldn't I have somebody to take care of things I can't do for myself? When Sonny Boy was alive things got done, but he's been gone now for a while."

"I understand how important a male presence can be."

Tootsie looked up at Mama thoughtfully; it was clear that she'd come to a decision. "Does Abe or that man from Columbia also want to talk with Stone?"

"I'm going to talk to Abe first thing tomorrow morning and suggest that he pick Stone up for questioning," Mama said evenly.

Fear flickered in Tootsie's eyes, as if she suddenly understood what Mama told her would mean for the teenager she'd taken into her bed. "I suppose I can get in touch with Stone, tell him you want to talk to him," she muttered.

Mama nodded, then motioned to me that it was time for us to leave.

"I wonder whether Brenda knew that her mother was sleeping with Stone," I said to Mama as I made a fresh pot of coffee and she prepared a salad.

"Brenda knew something that caused her to get herself killed," Mama answered.

"That boy might have killed three people already—It might be a good idea to call Abe to have Stone picked up for questioning tonight."

Mama nodded, then glanced at the clock. It was nearly ten o'clock. "It's late, I'll call him first thing tomorrow morning."

My father and Cliff hadn't come home yet from playing cards. While I cleaned the kitchen, Mama took a long hot bath and dressed in a comfortable pair of pajamas. Once I'd done my chores, I did the same thing.

My parents had remodeled the back of the house so that their kitchen and family room, with floor-to-ceiling windows, opened onto a backyard garden. The abundance of glass gave a panoramic view of the roses, azaleas, and annuals that bordered a chain-link fence. My mother and I sat drinking peppermint tea.

The telephone rang.

Mama was sitting on the couch, the chair closest to the phone. She picked it up, listened. A quizzical expression passed over her face. She placed the phone back on its receiver. "There was an odd breathy silence, then the person hung up without saying anything," she told me.

"Your first obscene phone call," I told her as I got up to go back into the kitchen to turn on the kettle again. I wanted a second cup of tea.

As I stood, the lights in our whole house blanked out.

The house was plunged into darkness. Fortunately, the moon shone through the window, and in a few seconds our eyes grew accustomed to the dark.

Mama stood, then walked to me. "I suppose we'd better go to bed. The lights will probably come back on before James and Cliff get back."

The words weren't out of her mouth when we saw a shadow slip through the gate.

Seconds later, we heard the first gunshot. The glass in front of where we stood shattered.

Mama and I dropped to the floor. My stomach contracted in a tight knot, my heart banged, my hands tingled. I must have leaped quite a distance, because I found myself inside the foyer, not far from the front door. Mama wasn't at my side.

"Mama!" I called out, my heart pounding out of control.

The shooter fired again, shattering more glass.

"It's Stone," Mama called back. "I expected to hear from him before the night was over."

"You expected that nut to try to shoot us?"

"I didn't think he'd be this cowardly, but I expected he'd want to get rid of us before I talked to Abe."

"And how did you plan for us to handle him?"

"I expected James and Cliff would be home before now."

I came up on my knees, trying to see her. "Well, we're on our own. He's got a clear shot from all the glass in the windows and the sliding door. Come into the foyer with me."

"I don't dare move."

"Where are you?"

"Behind the couch. If I move, he'll see me and hit me for sure."

Another shot, this bullet tearing through another window. We were trapped. If we didn't do something soon we would die.

"I'm going to try to get outside, go get help."

"For God's sake, Simone, be careful."

"Yeah," I said as I scooted backward to the front door, eased my hand along the doorframe until I touched the knob. Before I opened the door, I heard a growl and then a scream. My father's dog had attacked the shooter and was tearing at his flesh. Midnight had saved our lives.

EPILOGUE

When the wind blew in a certain direction, the aroma of spareribs on the charcoal grill overpowered Mama's zesty coleslaw, corn on the cob, baked beans, sliced tomatoes, sweetened iced tea, and deep-dish apple pie.

Six weeks had passed since Stone tried to kill us, since my father's dog, Midnight, had attacked the boy and saved our lives.

When he was arrested, Stone admitted that he'd killed Brenda, although the physical evidence Lew Hunter had collected was enough to convict him even if he hadn't confessed.

Stone also killed Kitty Sharp, he told Abe and Lew, because she was the person who told Brenda that he was the school's drug pusher. Kitty was a casual user who allowed her habit to become known to students, kids who told Brenda that she partied with them. Brenda wrote the letter to the school board. Kitty, out of fear, had told Brenda that Stone was the person she needed to finger. Brenda called SLED, and under Lew's direction, she'd tried to get him to reveal where he got the drugs.

Stone also confessed to killing old man Elliott because he started telling people that he thought it was strange that Stone spent so much time at Tootsie's house after Brenda was killed. Tootsie tried to get Stone to go home to keep people from talking and it angered the boy.

Tootsie's story was that she knew Stone was the killer, that she tried to stop him, that she feared for her own life, that Stone vowed he would kill her too if she turned him in.

She denied supplying Stone with drugs. A search warrant of her house and garage found the black Jaguar and a little cocaine, but nothing that suggested the level of drugs Stone was involved in pushing.

A few weeks later, however, fate took a hand.

Victor Powell, Stella Hope's stepfather, was fingered by a police informant as a big-time dealer who was trying to set up a gang of students in a town about the size of Otis not twenty miles outside of Columbia. Powell was arrested and when SLED searched his house they found letters from Tootsie, letters that kept him updated about the murders Stone was committing in Otis. Faced with this evidence, Tootsie admitted that she was the one running drugs in the high school and that Victor was her supplier.

Mama never got an opportunity to talk to Clyde Hicks, the boy everyone initially suspected was Brenda's murderer. The young man died when he hit a deer, riding his motorcycle without a helmet only a half mile from his home.

Midnight became a permanent houseguest. When it's time to go to sleep, he now has a very nice bed made for him in our kitchen.

The reason for the barbecue tonight was a celebration for Mama cracking the mask of innocence Tootsie adopted, a mask that hid how the woman used Stone to sell drugs to high school students.

Cliff and I came home for the occasion. Festive colored lights designed to keep bugs at bay were strung across the entire backyard. The windows shattered by Stone's bullets had all been replaced. The night was warm with only a slight breeze.

The guests were: Abe, Rick, and Lew; Hattie; Pepper and Zack Garvey; Agatha and Gertrude; Carrie, Annie Mae, and Sarah; Ray Raisin; and Coal and three or four more of my father's buddies.

Daddy, a beer in one hand, and a brush in another, spread his secret sauce on the meat. The sound of soft jazz permeated the air.

The rest of the food was on the table. Finally the

ribs were ready. My father lifted the pan of ribs and sashayed with them past our noses.

It was heavenly.

Daddy looked at my mother and winked. "Candi, baby, your old man has done his thing this time!"

Mama smiled.

ACKNOWLEDGMENTS

Thanks to the many readers who contacted me to share their delight in becoming acquainted with Mama. I am pleased so many people enjoyed visiting Mama (Candi), Simone, James, Cliff, and their family and friends in Otis, South Carolina. My sincere desire is that Mama will continue to provide her fans with years of delightful and intriguing mysteries.

ABOUT THE AUTHOR

NORA DELOACH is an Orlando, Florida, native presently living in Decatur, Georgia. She is married and the mother of three.